MW01243383

FINALLY
His

Bedtime Stories, Volume Two

ELIZABETH SaFLEUR

Elizabeth SaFleur LLC
PO Box 6395
Charlottesville, VA 22906
Elizabeth@ElizabethSaFleur.com
www.ElizabethSaFleur.com

Edited by Olivia Kalb
Proofread by Claire Milto
Cover design by LJ Designs
ISBN: 978-1-949076-54-7

FINALLY, HIS

By Elizabeth SaFleur

A collection of Elite Doms of Washington novelettes

Finally, His

Exploring her darker longings was the deal. Falling for him—fast and hard—wasn't.

For years Colette harbored secret desires—ones that were forbidden and dangerous. When a man resurfaces from her past, he offers a chance to explore her darker imaginings. She didn't expect to fall for him—hard, fast and irrevocably.

The Portrait

Being loved by someone was supposed to be simple, natural. But what if that someone is desired by everyone?

For years Eric secretly loved Alexander from afar. Everyone else did, too. But Eric got lucky. Love bloomed between them—and a third, Rebecca. But old insecurities continue to rise, threatening it all.

When Darkness Calls

Even perfect love can't conquer some nightmares—or so she believed.

Charlotte's past is ugly by no fault of her own. Her Master will do anything to finally rid her of her hideous memories, and when he finally calls on their Club Accendos family she must make a choice: Confront the worst of them or possibly lose him forever.

.

TABLE OF CONTENTS

ACKNOWLEDGEMENTS

Dear Reader,

This book is a work of fiction, not reality. My characters operate in a compressed time frame. A real-world scenario involves getting to know one another more extensively than my characters do before engaging in BDSM activities. Please learn as much as you can before trying any activity you read about in erotic fiction. Talk to people in your local BDSM group. Nearly every community has one. Get to know people slowly, and always be careful. Share your hopes, dreams and fears with anyone before playing with them, have a safeword and share it with your Dom or Domme (they can't read your mind), use protection, and have a safe-call or other backup in place. Remember: Safe, Sane and Consensual. Or no play. May you find that special person to honor and love you the way you wish. You deserve that.

XO ~Elizabeth

Finally, His

Formerly titled *Called to the Dean's Office*

Chapter One

Colette had crept along the edges of the ballroom all evening, taking in the scenes one by one—spanking, flogging, rope bondage. It wasn't until she and her friend Charlotte stopped to watch a fire scene that she first noticed him.

"He's most definitely interested," Charlotte whispered in her ear. "Care for an introduction?"

The man's eyes—dark and glittering in the low light behind a black mask—were so familiar Colette's chest ached with a memory trying to surface. Yet when would she have met anyone from that world?

She swallowed and fiddled with the lace edge of her corset. She enjoyed his interest, but what could she say to the mysterious stranger? She could barely believe she stood in a BDSM play party at all.

Colette had often passed the place, a large mansion,

half-hidden by overgrown ivy and boxwoods behind the large, scrolled gates, and wondered who lived there. Now, she knew—the silver-haired Alexander Rockingham, whom she'd met as soon as she'd stepped into the front entrance, an oval portico filled with fresh flowers.

He'd taken her hand and smiled warmly at her before sharing the rules of his home-sometimes-club.

No one would engage her unless she indicated interest.

Ask as many questions as she liked.

And whenever she wanted to leave, she could. In fact, they had a car waiting for her should she choose to go.

Leaving was out of the question. For a decade, she'd woken in the middle of the night with wisps of dreams floating just out of her grasp—leaving behind a strange desire. A hand on the back of her neck. An overload of sensation. Fear mixed with something wickedly delicious. She'd always woken from those dreams like she had a secret life waiting to live—one that was forbidden and dangerous.

Or just plain crazy. She could be that, too.

A long sizzle followed by a blue flame arching to the domed ceiling had her shuddering, and she took two steps to the left to distance herself from the heat. The man mirrored her movements. No mistaking it. He was tracking her as if he were a hunter—and she was the prey. A tendril of heat crawled up her inner thighs at the mere thought.

She'd walked into a room worthy of an erotic Pinterest board, where women's skin glowed like the surface of a pearl, and men's abs were so toned they cast shadows. Yet this man standing across the ballroom hadn't ripped his eyes from her. *Her*.

Charlotte placed a hand on her wrist. "He won't approach you, but if he's making you uncomfortable—"

"No, not at all." On the contrary, the idea of being chased—and then caught—was thrilling.

Perhaps he'd yank at her corset strings, desperate to get her out of them. Or he'd rip her fishnet stockings with his bare hands.

Maybe he'd do both.

Colette startled once more when the sizzle of flames cut through her trance. The woman, clad in a black lace bodysuit, ran her hand over her submissive's back and left a trail of blue flame dancing across his skin.

Colette's admirer on the other side of the scene hadn't flinched. Rather, he stood tall and comfortable, his eyes drilling into her.

She turned to her friend. "Um, if I was interested, how does that work?"

Charlotte gave her a knowing smile. "You would simply walk up to him. Or I could send a message."

"Oh, no. I'd feel like I'm in high school all over again." Or worse, college, where she'd nursed a significant crush on a particular Medieval History professor. How odd she thought of him then.

As an English major, she didn't need to know the ins and outs of the Norman Conquest and the War of the Roses. Yet, there she was, three days a week, surrounded by equally besotted female students, ridiculously attracted to a man with dark, swoony eyes—similar to her secret follower.

She was a sucker for dark and swoony.

Charlotte took her arm and guided her to the next scene.

Across the ballroom, the man moved with them. His gaze continued to bear down on Colette, his interest obvious. She could scarcely look away herself.

How bad would it be to just talk to him? But ask him ... what? *Come here often? Live around here? Want to give me my first adult spanking?*

His gaze lazily drifted from her face, down her neck, to the exposed skin above her corset, and continued down her torso to her legs. Her knees quivered. His gaze then snapped back to her face. Was that a smile on his lips?

"Actually," Colette turned to Charlotte, "it's okay if he does. I mean, approaches me."

Charlotte gave her a small smile "Good choice. He's quite ... something. He's a good teacher." She turned her face to him and cocked her head.

He nodded once at her and began to move their way. *Holy shit.* That fast? She could use a little time—like maybe a week at a spa, a month or two to tone up her butt and thighs.

Just breathe. She adjusted the light blue mask on her face, the color indicating she was new. A neon sign might have been more comfortable to wear, given she was only one of two people in the room sporting the color.

His strides ate up the expensive Oriental carpeting. When he was a mere twelve inches from her, her neck craned to look up into his face. Now, so close to his glittering eyes, every nerve in her body lit up like the sun. Her heart thundered against her ribs, and her teeth grabbed her bottom lip—probably more to have something to do rather than chatter.

"Hello." His voice matched his eyes—deep and assured.

With a small wink, Charlotte scooted away, and the room constricted, narrowing down to him as if all the people around them had been pushed away by invisible hands.

"Hi. I'm …" Why was she having such trouble forming words? As a foreign language translator, she was usually much quicker with them—in four languages.

"Colette. Yes, I know."

Of course, he knew. Everyone in the room likely had a dossier on her already—something with big letters that said, "*Look, but don't touch*."

Alexander's club application was akin to filling out a college application—and one that only allowed her entry to tonight's introduction party. Nothing beyond. Apparently, to join the club officially, one must have a background check worthy of the CIA.

The masked man held out a hand, which she took.

Warm flesh engulfed her hand. "Enjoying yourself?"

She nodded. Enjoying wasn't the word she'd use, but it'd do.

"Anything in particular catch your eye?" His hand kept possession of hers.

Okay, small talk was underrated anyway. "I'm not sure yet. But nothing I've seen has me running for the hills—yet." She tried to sound light, flirty. Instead, her voice came out thin and little more than a squeak.

"I'm glad to hear it." He studied her face. "You look beautiful tonight, Colette. But then, you always did." He flipped her hand over and pressed a small card into her palm. "Think about it."

He then released his handhold and strode away.

Wait a minute. Always did? She glanced down at the little card he'd given her. It read: *Griffin Miles Storm.*

Her brain froze along with every part of her body. He couldn't be.

On the back, he'd written a note in large-scrolled handwriting. *My office. Thursday. 12 noon.*

No address. But he didn't need to give one, did he? She knew exactly where his office was. Knew who *he* was.

Holy. Shit. She glanced around, her eyes searching for him, a man she hadn't believed she'd ever see again.

Charlotte was by her side in seconds. She squeezed Colette's elbow. "It appears he's very interested indeed."

"He gave me his card." She enclosed both hands over it, almost afraid to look at it again.

"Oh, that means the ball is in your court. And if you do contact him, know it'll likely be the last time."

"Last time?"

"The ball. Your court." Charlotte smiled at her. "Master Griffin is, well, a man who's always in charge. It's better if you two talk."

Adrenaline spiked so hard she could barely breathe.

Charlotte's brows furrowed. "Hey, are you okay? You know you don't ever have to—"

"No." She forced a smile on her face. "I'm fine. I just can't believe …"

"Oh, I know. It's exciting, isn't it?" Charlotte whisper-squealed in her ear. "You're finally taking the first step."

She should have never shared her fantasies with Charlotte. Her friend swore she'd never run into anyone she knew at Club Accendos, and identities were strictly hidden at introductory parties. *Ha!* Colette was just handed a stiff business card by someone she'd never, ever believed she'd see again—Griffin Storm, her Medieval History professor.

Chapter Two

The opaque glass window of the door rattled under Colette's knuckles. As she waited for someone to answer, she drank in the name etched there—**Griffin Miles Storm, Dean, Arts & Humanities**. He'd been promoted since she'd last stood in his presence—or, should she say, trembled in his classroom?

She swallowed as if that would help stuff down the butterflies threatening to take flight in her throat.

In all her twenty-six years, Colette had plenty of practice dealing with things that made her belly flutter, and she prided herself on overcoming them. Like when she was six years old on the playground, and Billy Turner dared her to swing herself so high the chain links slacked. Or when she'd gotten her first translation job and the snotty Italian diplomat tested her by throwing out sex terms to see how she'd handle it. She'd blushed hard but recited the correct words.

The only place she'd ever failed at displaying much courage was with Griffin Storm. The man had occupied her shockingly graphic, filthy imagination all through college. He'd look at her in class with such drop-to-your-knees intensity that she'd weaken to the point of being mute.

That night's introduction showed things hadn't much changed with him. Just recalling how his dark eyes blazed her way made her want to flee like a rabbit being chased by a wolf—a rabbit that wanted to be caught. That was before she knew who he was.

Only, if she'd left, she'd be back to where she started—being fixed up by well-meaning friends with accountants and lawyers who talked about work promotions and beach vacations at the Outer Banks.

She didn't see Griffin Storm standing on the beach with a Budweiser in his hand. Rather, he held a flogger in a dark ballroom.

She gently rapped on the door once more, that time a little louder.

"Enter." The deep male voice that rumbled through the glass door was unmistakable. It *was* him. Seeing him the other night wasn't a dream.

She turned the knob, stepped inside, and willed herself to keep breathing as she caught sight of the man behind the large oak desk.

He stared down at a folder, a curl of dark hair falling into his face. She cleared her throat, and his lashes lifted. She nearly swooned. Did he have to have such beautiful eyes? Soulful, liquidy-dark, and fierce?

She managed to get the door closed, the click echoing in her brain like a ping-pong ball in an arcade machine.

She turned to face him. "Dean Storm," she managed to peep out.

He rose so slowly it was as if he was unfolding, growing taller. "Hello, Colette. Sit." He pointed to a wooden chair in front of his desk.

She quickly took a seat and set her bag down next to her. She smoothed her skirt as if that would lengthen the cotton. Funny, it'd never seemed too short before. Now, she paraded too much skin.

"You asked to meet with me?"

"There was no asking involved." He sat on the edge of his desk before her. "Interesting to see you at Club Accendos the other evening."

The man got straight to the point, didn't he? "Yes. I was just … accompanying my friend, Charlotte." And then darting out of there like a scared rabbit once she'd realized who he was.

"I hope I wasn't why you ran away."

"I didn't run away." More like stumbled out of Accendos, a few people rushing to help her to the promised waiting car. Charlotte insisted on going with her, and she'd had to endure her friend's constant questioning about whether anything bad had happened between her and Griffin. Apparently, if so, the club owner would have a "*conniption fit the size of a tsunami.*"

Colette forced the lump down her throat. "My attendance was … an experiment. I mean, Charlotte needed someone to go with her, and—"

"No, she didn't. She's quite comfortable at Accendos."

Busted.

A slight smile threatened to form on his face. "Her Master and I are friends."

So, so busted.

He crossed his arms. "Did someone say something to you? Something happen?"

"No." *Liar. You happened, Dean Storm.*

He uncrossed his arms and sighed. "Then it was me. Had I known my card would elicit such a response, I would never have offered it."

Was this meeting an apology? Remorse? Neither felt right coming from him. Over the years, she'd believed he, with his gorilla-sized energy, would never stoop to regrets.

She, on the other hand, had always regretted not being braver about her sexual proclivities. The other night was supposed to be the beginning of calling up some courage around the kind of relationship she sought. Showing up at his office was even a step further. But now? *Scared rabbit intact.*

"Colette?" His gaze continued to sear her skin. Or perhaps just being that close to him caused her body to heat up as if standing before a live fire, which made her a *roasted rabbit*.

She shrugged. "You took me by surprise, that's all. I attended on a whim." What was she saying? She couldn't just say, "I wanted you to catch me," but now? Her fingers trembled. They wouldn't still.

"You signed quite the NDA to be there." He shifted a little, and who knew the rustle of his pants legs would make her inner thighs quiver? "You waited weeks to be let in, even just for an introductory talk. I'd say it was more than a whim."

"I was curious." *Curious* didn't even begin to touch her imaginings around what people did at Accendos. And the thought of what *he* did there?

He leaned toward her, and a warm, male scent wafted her way. She squirmed a little in her seat as his proximity woke up different parts of her body, particularly one section between her legs.

"Anyone who ends up at Accendos is more than curious," he said. "You can tell me the truth. In fact, I insist on it. Are you seeking someone to explore certain … longings?"

Oh, he truly did get straight to the heart of things— or in her case, her physical desires. "Yes. I've played … a little." If she counted being handcuffed to the bed by a past boyfriend—exactly twice. "So, if you think I'd ever out you—"

"I'm not concerned about that. NDA, remember? I am rather interested to know, however, if you were glad to see me."

She couldn't answer him. Instead, she chewed on her bottom lip. The answer to his question would be too embarrassing. Glad? How about unable to contain herself with glee? She was scared out of her mind—so out of her depth—but she'd crossed some line that made her a little giddy inside, like maybe she was headed in the right direction for once.

"Colette?"

"I was." She'd spent the entire night tossing and turning in bed, trying to piece together some composure over the thought of Professor Storm … *doing things to her.*

He cocked his head, and his eyes glanced down to her fingers curled under her hem. His lashes lifted once more—and there it was. That look that had made her want to prostrate herself before him every time he singled her out in class six years ago. Hell, every time he'd glanced her way. He may be eleven years older than she, but that only ratcheted up her fantasies.

His last name, Storm, suited him. His aura wasn't calm. The air swirled around him as if it was destined to circle him and only him. It was downright unsettling—and she loved how it made her body thrum with attention.

Unable to stare into his eyes any longer, she studied her fingers, now twisting in her lap. Then she let her gaze wander around his office. Couch. Diplomas on the wall. Anything to distract herself from the maelstrom of feelings arising in her.

Rough fingers scooped under her chin and lifted her face. "When you were in my class, did you ever imagine me doing things to you?"

Oh, Jesus. *Things?* How about a library's worth of *things* that he'd already done to her inside her own head? If they spilled out to the world, she'd have to wear a permanent warning label: *Woman steeped in smutty debauchery.*

He arched an eyebrow, probably because her mouth had gone slack due to his touch. "Sometimes." *Please don't make me voice it.*

"I won't tolerate a second of denial from you, little Colette." He dropped his hand, and one side of his lips quirked up. "Isn't that why you wore a skirt? For me to do something to you?"

"I often wear skirts," she said quickly.

"I remember. And lucky me." He rose.

She was only this ridiculously awkward around him. Truth told, she'd been with plenty of men. Let them take her, lick her between her legs, thrust themselves inside her. None of them interested her for more than a few dates.

But Griffin? The things she would let him do didn't even have names yet. He could own her. His very existence was an unfair advantage over her. Only she wanted him to have that power, didn't she?

He rounded his desk. The scrape of wood sounded as he pulled open the top drawer of his desk. He placed a thin dime store ruler, a steel pointer stick she recognized from some of his past lectures, and a bamboo backscratcher on the desk. He lined them up side by side.

She stared at them.

He stepped from behind the desk, leaned against the wall alongside a bookcase. "You can leave anytime. We can forget we saw one another at all."

Forget? She'd need a lobotomy, and even then, she wasn't sure that would work. Griffin Storm asking her if she wished he'd do *things* and providing … implements?

He was taunting her. Yes, that was exactly what he was doing. Did she mind? She didn't mind. Not at all. It was a game—a thrilling chase.

She stood. "I suppose we could."

"Forget each other? Or do something?"

"Something," she said far too quickly.

"Then choose," he said. "Take your time. I don't have another meeting for an hour."

An hour. Did Colette want to be with Griffin Storm for an hour? Doing things to her with the pointer? Or the bamboo scratcher? No, she wanted him to spank her with the ruler until her ass was on fire, and then he'd …

A sound had come from his direction. He'd growled. Was it because her hand had found its way to the ruler? She'd been running her index finger up and down the edge without realizing it. He wanted her to pick this one, hadn't he?

She lifted the cheap wooden stick, little black hash marks indicating inches.

He pushed off the wall and held out his hand, and she placed it in his open palm.

"And what should I do with this?" He lifted it high in his hand.

"Whatever you want."

By how his lips quirked, he seemed pleased by her answer. She worked for herself, so it was easy to break for an hour—or two. In fact, she could spend a whole day with him if he wanted.

"Put this in your purse." He handed her the ruler. "If you wish for me to guide you in this world—"

"I do."

His face hardened but then softened. "I want you to think about what you want. But even more importantly, what you don't want. I want a written list of things you do not consent to. Do you understand?"

He wanted her limits. "I can tell you now." She could recite them that second or run home and retrieve the written list she'd completed years ago, which was safely hidden in a box under her bed …

He slowly shook his head and then rounded his desk. "One week. Then we'll see."

A whiny part of her squeaked loud in her soul. Seven days would also be an eternity.

"Okay." Such an awful, do-nothing word, but it was the only one she had at the moment.

"See you then. Same day, same time."

He was serious. A week? Was he kidding?

He stared down at his laptop screen. She'd been dismissed.

"Oh, and Colette." He peered up at her. "Put the ruler on your nightstand. I want you to look at it every night, but you are not to use it on yourself."

Oh, great. That was all she could think about now, how it might feel if she slapped her butt with it. She nodded in affirmation. Her imagination, however? That wouldn't be contained.

"Bring it back to me next week, along with your limits list."

"Will you use it then?" She promptly flushed from head to toe.

He chuckled, slapped his laptop shut, and dropped himself to his chair. "We'll see."

Her crotch, already burning with desire, fired like a kiln.

Chapter Three

Colette pulled at the hem of her skirt at the rustle of paper as Griffin turned the page. He cleared his throat, peering up at her and then back down to the paper. What did he think of her limits list? Could she ask?

She'd spent all week revising and changing it—and ended up keeping her original one. Her libido—which was on *fire* since he'd pressed that card into her hand at Accendos—was not a good judge around such matters. Her desire screamed *yes, yes, yes* to anything her mind conjured up.

At night, she'd wake from her dreams about Griffin with her hand between her legs.

During the day, her mind drifted to what he was doing—and if he was *doing* anyone.

She'd then start the process all over again—an endless cycle of thinking about him, wanting him.

The fact that he now fingered the ruler she'd returned to him and twirled it in his hand wasn't helping stop the tide of desire. At all.

At night, she'd put the thing on her nightstand as directed. During the day, she'd carried it around in her purse as if he'd suddenly call and request her presence. A girl had to be prepared.

"Hmm." He glanced up at her again. "So, Dante?"

At the last minute, she'd put a safeword at the bottom. "Yes. Unless you think it's silly."

"Nothing silly about it." His chair thunked upright. He set the list down but kept hold of the ruler. "Stand up."

She rose to stand and hoped her legs weren't shaking too much.

"I'm glad you wore a skirt again."

The fact that he'd have easier access wasn't the only reason she chose it. He'd noticed her outfit the last time she'd quaked in his office, so hell yes, she was wearing another one.

He rounded to the front, and her thighs squeezed together as if that would stop the ache rising there by his approach.

"I remember that look."

Her heart thudded against her ribs, and she swallowed.

"The way your eyes followed me as I paced."

Gah. Had she been that obvious back then? Of course, she had. She and every other female in the room.

"You were quite passionate about your subject," she said.

One side of his mouth quirked up. "What else did you

think about me?"

Admitting her crush would be humiliating, perhaps, but what did she have to lose? He would think she was silly. "I'm embarrassed to say what I thought about you."

"Desiring someone isn't anything to be embarrassed about—especially as an adult."

"Which we both are." Good, her voice was stronger.

"We are. And we both have certain needs. I know now what you don't want, but what are you hoping for?"

You. "A teacher. Will you? I mean, be mine?" *Oh. My. God.* She even sounded like a teenager with an elephant-sized crush. Her face dropped to her hands, now nearly white from twisting her fingers together.

His hand reached out and stilled her twisting fingers. "Look at me."

The knot in her throat was pushed down with a lot of effort—almost as much as lifting her gaze to his face. She hadn't expected to see kindness there. It almost made her want to cry.

"Yes. I can do that. But I'll require you to honor my directions and commands. That's what I need."

"Like not using the ruler."

"Among other things. You enjoyed following my order?"

"Yes." In a strange way, she had. It was like she knew what to *do*. No thought, no bargaining with herself. It was … black and white. And she'd anticipated the smile he now wore when she could stand before him and say she'd done what he'd asked.

"Very good. I certainly enjoy giving them. And, if you

do obey, you'll enjoy the rewards. If not, you are free to leave."

"I don't want to leave."

"What do you want?"

"To learn." She took in a shaky breath. "To submit to you." Wow, she really said the words aloud. A huge weight lifted from her chest. Maybe that was why following his next command was shockingly easy.

"Bend over the desk. Ass up."

Oh, fast. That didn't stop her from flattening her torso on the desk with such speed she shocked herself. The scent of manilla folder filled her nostrils as her cheek rested on a cool, old-fashioned ink blotter.

His hand rested on one hip while fingers of the other trailed up her thighs and lifted her skirt. She shuddered hard.

"I agree to mentor you. We'll see if this lifestyle suits you."

If she was good enough? Or perhaps he couldn't stop being the teacher and she the student.

His voice washed over her once more. "You say *Dante*, and all this will end. No repercussions. No questions. It'll just stop."

"Don't stop," she said. Because his fingers trailing up her skin? She'd dreamed of that exact touch a thousand times.

He chuckled. "But you will if you need to. Now, lift."

Her hips rose without a second thought, allowing him to raise her skirt until it bunched around her waist. She settled back down on the skirt's cushion under her hip bones.

Then ...

Her whole world stopped because his hands were on both of her thighs. She widened her stance, earning another low murmur from his throat. It only made her want to split her legs farther apart, but his hands held her fast.

Hot breath touched her panties—and shot straight through to her clit.

"Do you know how many times I imagined bending you over this desk?"

He had? Her breath was so loud against the desk blotter.

"Lifting your little skirts. Pushing your panties aside."

"Thank you." Jesus, her voice shook.

He chuckled. The scuff of his shoe sounded as he rose, and then a sharp crack and sting spread across her flesh. *Oh, shit, that hurt.*

"Thank you, what?" he asked.

"Thank you, Sir."

Another whack and a bleat left her throat. She swallowed hard as saliva pooled in her mouth. His fingers touched the fire on her ass, and she squirmed.

With no more words, he landed more blows on her flesh with the ruler, the smacking sound filling the room. Did people in the hallway hear? She could call "Dante"— would that put her in heaven or hell?

He rained slaps on her ass until she disappeared into sensation and need. Her crotch pressed against the edge of the desk. If only she could rub up against something, satisfy that aching burn …

A clatter sounded behind her as if he dropped the ruler. Then she was separating from the desk. He righted her and turned her to face him.

She panted, but he looked as composed as ever. He swiped a thumb under her eye and brought it to his lips. He licked her tears from the pad of his finger. "Mmm, I always did like sweet with salty."

She hadn't even known her eyes had leaked.

His hand curled around the base of her neck and crushed his mouth against hers. His tongue forced its way inside. If she thought she'd been kissed before, she'd been sorely mistaken.

His lips were strong, and his tongue breached her mouth with no hesitation. For long minutes, he possessed her that way, and soon, his arms held her up because standing was impossible.

"Take off your panties," he said into her mouth.

She steadied her feet to stand on her own accord and then hooked her thumbs in her panties. They dropped to her ankles with no protest.

He breathed heavily into her mouth. "Leave the skirt up."

Oh, wow. He would see everything. He stepped backward. Yes, everything as cool air touched her bruised lips and crotch. The hot fire grew inside her as his gaze landed *there*. His lips inched up into a slow smile.

He held out a palm. "Your panties."

She bent down and retrieved them. They were soaked. She balled up the scrap of cotton as best she could and placed them in his palm.

"I'm keeping these. Next time, you won't wear them, will you?"

Okay, this was it. She could say "no" and never see him

again. But who would she be kidding? "Yes. I mean, no, I won't wear them. Sir."

He seemed pleased. "Lower your skirt."

Once she did, she didn't know what to do next. Should she leave?

"Are you okay?" His brow furrowed a bit. He reached over and swiped his hand along her jawline. A tear escaped her eye, and she batted at it, embarrassed.

His hand circled her wrist and pulled her closer to him. "Never hide those from me."

She couldn't if she tried.

His arms went around her and pulled her into his chest. With one arm binding him to her, he reached to his desk and retrieved a bottle of water. "Drink."

She took it in both hands and tipped it to her lips. "Thank you."

"It's my job to take care of you as you explore." Another caress of his hand alongside her head left her speechless. His tenderness was so unexpected. "It's my pleasure to do so."

"I'm good, really," she said quickly. She wouldn't be a burden.

"Hmmm. Let's sit for a bit." He pulled her toward the black couch against the one bare wall. How many women had he lured to his couch?

She sat, but he pushed her down, so she lay across his lap, cheek on his thigh, her legs curled under her.

He played with her hair. "Beautiful, little Colette."

Her head shook a "no" involuntarily.

"It wasn't a question," he said.

She sat up—not quite believing the moment. No words came from her lips, though. He thought she was *beautiful*. At that moment, if she could have crawled under his skin, she'd have done it.

"How are you feeling?"

"Good. Better than good, actually."

His gaze raked over her whole body. "Tomorrow. Twelve noon. Can you make that?"

She nodded.

"Good." He rose, holding out his hand to her. Okay, guess she was leaving. She picked up her purse and met him at the doorway. Thank God the hallway was empty.

Before she could slip outside, he grasped her hand. "No visiting Accendos. If you do, it will be with me."

A trickle of wet trailed down her leg at the very thought. "Yes, Sir."

His eyes raked down her body to her feet, and she pressed her thighs together as if that would keep him from seeing her juices on display.

"Good answer," he said. "I look forward to more of those responses," his chin tipped down toward her legs, "from you."

Oh, God. Fantasies, move over. Reality had moved in.

"And you are not to come until I say so."

She'd turned every shade known to the color Pantone scale because she, of course, had planned to ride a stallion-sized vibrator as soon as she could. His spanking raised a raging need, which she supposed had been the point.

"Do you understand?" he asked.

"Yes." *Dammit.*

"Gold star." One kiss to the forehead, and then she was shut out into the hallway.

Chapter Four

The next morning, Colette returned to his office at her lunch hour as directed—as she had every day that week.

On Monday, he'd programmed his number into her phone. She was to send him any question she had—anytime, day or night—and he would answer. He then spanked her, kissed her, cuddled her on that damned couch, and told her she wasn't to come until he told her she could. He'd texted her late that night and asked how she was. His attention only made her want to come more.

Tuesday, Wednesday, and Thursday were a repeat. Spank. Kiss. Orders.

By Friday morning, she woke up pissed. An inferno raged between her legs, and there was no way she'd make it through translating *The Elements and Architecture of Molecules* from English to Italian without an orgasm that would take her head off. And it was all because of him.

She'd texted Griffin with a simple question.

<<Am I ever going to be able to come again?>>

She wasn't that forward—ever. But she had an entire book to translate by the end of the month, and at the rate she was going, the language would be dead to the world by the time she finished.

His answer back was immediate.

<<Perhaps.>>

Bastard. Maybe the man was a sadist. How quickly he went from the most amazing man on earth to the devil.

By Friday's lunch hour, she felt like she might kill someone. She was a cauldron of need. A glory hole of heat. A sun burning a path wherever she tread.

Had she always been so … physical?

Had she ever bared so much skin to someone in under a week's time?

Had she ever believed she'd let her dirty desires out to play?

It was all Griffin Miles Storm's fault. He had to show up at Accendos, stare at her hard across a ballroom full of moans and acres of gorgeous skin and turn her into his blob of someone-fuck-me-already.

Only she didn't want just *someone.* She needed one man with dark, glittery eyes who asked her—no, *told* her— to come to him. She had. She'd presented a limits list, had told him what she wanted, asked him to be her teacher, abandoned wearing panties under her skirts, let him gaze at her with those tender yet stormy eyes, and then she'd agreed to keep coming back to him for more.

Maybe she couldn't do this—whatever *this* was—

because when he laid her over his desk again on Friday, a position she was quite used to by then, she burst into tears.

His hand rubbed her bare ass. "You're okay, little Colette."

"No, I'm not." She could say *Dante* and end the torment. Instead, she sobbed for long minutes. He rubbed her skin, murmuring to her. When she finally could contain herself, she snuffed up her nose. "I'm s-sorry."

"Nothing to be sorry about. What are those tears for?"

"You know."

He slapped her ass.

"I can't stop wanting … needing … I'm just so frustrated," she gritted out and turned her head to look at him.

"Good."

Good? Perhaps he was crazy? Most certainly sadistic. She tried to ease up, but his hand pushed her back down. "It means your desire was sustainable."

Sustainable. What an interesting word. She'd have used intolerable.

One thick brow arched. "You have a safeword."

"No," she cried out. "I don't want to use it." She let her tears and snot stain his ink blotter, evidence of her misery.

"But you will when you need to." His hands were suddenly gone from her. He'd stepped back. "Safewords aren't used for manipulating what you want to happen, but at the very least, you call it when you feel in danger."

She twisted more so she could see his whole face.

His eyes glittered under the fluorescent lights. "Rise."

She pushed herself up and turned to face him.

He grasped her waist and hauled her up to sit on the desk. "First lesson. Tell me specifically what you want."

"I need to come."

"That wasn't so hard, was it?"

She rolled her eyes. His hand grasped her chin, and his face hardened. *Uh-oh.* More tears leaked down her cheeks.

"This week was horrible." Oh, God, she sniveled.

He nodded. "Now, you'll have to beg me."

Her mouth slacked. His hand left her. She choked back the anxiety rising in her throat as his dark eyes stared down at her … waiting.

His lips thinned. "Beg me to make you come, Colette."

He was displeased with her. "Please?"

"Please what?"

"Please, let me come. I'll do anything." Well, not anything, but she was pretty damned close. Not enough? "Please, sir, please, please, please."

He nodded once. "Set your ass on the desk, spread your knees, and show me how much you need it."

Okay, it was his desk to ruin. She did what he asked, slowly widened her legs.

His gaze dropped to her between her legs—and he smiled. "Pink. Beautiful."

For so many years, she'd thought of herself like that – opening to him, being ready for him, accepting him. The reality, however, raised a mix of shame and need that made her entire body quake. The opposing urges to stop and continue warred inside her.

"Put both hands on either side of you, palms to the desk."

She swallowed but followed his orders. Her need won over any sense of indignity. She laid both palms down by her sides, which forced her to lean back as if she was offering herself to him. She was.

He wasted no time thrusting two fingers inside her, and she cried out.

His eyes stormed down at her. "This one time, I'm going to release you since you asked me so nicely. But let me be clear. Your orgasms belong to me. And only I say when you can have them."

She grasped her teeth between her lips and whimpered anew. She nodded vigorously—and his fingers widened into a V. God, the stretch felt amazing.

"You're doing so well, little Colette." He slowly pulled his fingers out and then pushed them back in. "You please me." His thumb pressed against her clit hard. "When you're being good."

She could have stifled her groan, but she didn't care to. He was *pleased*.

"I can do better," she breathed.

"Yes, you can. So, after today, you may beg, cry, and scream, but I will choose when and how you come. Do you understand?"

His fingers twisted, curled, and explored with such conviction she wondered if she'd ever be able to touch herself again and have it feel as good.

"Do. You. Understand?" He widened his fingers, and she gasped at the stretch.

She mewled and nodded once.

His lips turned up as his hand went to work on her.

It only took a minute for him to build to a rhythm, a pace just that side of too slow. She rocked her hips, pitched them forward, trying to capture more of those thick fingers moving in and out and in …

He tsked. "Trying to set the pace? Don't be ungrateful for what I offer."

She stilled though her body screamed for more. Her limbs oddly loosened but tightened, and so much heat built that her skin broke out in a sheen. His office filled with her pants—nothing new this last week.

"You're close, aren't you?" he asked.

Another nod because words were beyond her. His hand continued at a maddening pace, not slow, not fast. His eyes were transfixed on her pussy, wet sounds joining her breaths.

"Tell me when you're there." Light caught in his eyes, and every memory she had of that glint—from his pacing in a room smelling of chalk and old wood to the more recent leather and citrus of Club Accendos—got her right on the precipice.

"Oh, God. Now."

He thrust three fingers inside her, the deeper invasion sending her into spasms. Her mouth dropped to an O, and her spine curled inward to him. His arm snaked up her spine, and his large hand grasped the back of her neck.

Before her cry could be unleashed, he crushed her mouth to his.

Jesus, his lips were a godsend—taking all her frustration and her relief into him. She shuddered as wave after wave convulsed on his fingers. Nothing—*nothing*—had ever felt so good. Time, place, it was all meaningless in the crashing and burning inside her body.

When his mouth released her, his eyes smiled down at her. "Beautiful girl."

Her limbs were loose and elastic, and she gave him a watery smile. Out of habit, she shook her head at his compliment. She had her good days and bad days, but beautiful wasn't even remotely part of her good days.

He slid his fingers free of her, raised them to her mouth, and forced them inside. "Don't ever belittle yourself. Do you understand?"

She blinked.

"Suck them off and nod if you understand."

She nodded and ran her tongue all around, licking and cleaning herself off him.

When he pulled them free, he yanked her closer. "Of course, giving me a 'yes, Sir' also suffices." His smile was back. It was ridiculous the effect it had on her. Had she ever needed someone's approval that much?

"Thank you, Sir. And thank you for letting me …" She lowered her lashes. She worked with words, yet they seemed so distant. Perhaps because her tongue had relaxed fully for the first time in days. A sense of peace filled her where before there had been nothing but tension and anger.

He moved the hair from her face, the strands pulling away from her damp skin. "I'm strict but not cruel. You have my word on that."

She believed him—sort of.

"It's my job to test your limits. We might have gotten close to one today."

She sniffed and nodded vigorously. He released her,

too-cold air hitting her between her legs.

"But we can get closer still. There are great rewards to be had from delayed gratification."

"But you won't make me wait forever?"

"Forever is a very long time. Now, Saturday." He lifted an eyebrow. "You're free?"

She blinked. For him, she would be free for the rest of her life—even if they only had now. "Yes." She slowly pulled her thighs together, aware of the slickness she was about to leave on his desktop.

"Good. I'll reserve a room for us at Accendos. That is if you wish to continue."

Her cheeks lifted, and air filled her lungs. "Yes, please. Sir." She emphasized the last word.

"I'll pick you up at seven."

She nodded, and the pleasure in his eyes at her answer sealed her fate. She was his—at least for now.

She had to savor it. He agreed only to mentor her—not take her on. He wasn't her boyfriend or even really her lover. Perhaps if she were perfect, though, he'd continue a while.

She straightened herself up and eased off the desk. Oh, yeah, he would need a new ink blotter.

He didn't seem to mind, only pulling her skirt down her legs.

He straightened, his dark eyes bearing down on her. "Expect to beg more."

Chapter Five

If Colette had let her imagination play unhindered and without boundaries, she still wouldn't have guessed all that Club Accendos offered.

Two men met them in the entry portico to escort them through the club. She huddled into Griffin's arm. He tucked her close as they strode down the long hallway to the Library. He couldn't seem to stop touching her. His hand on her thigh on the ride over, the hand on the small of her back easing her forward on Accendos' walkway, then holding her hand, his large palm on the back of her neck the second they stepped inside—she loved it all.

Thick carpet muffled their footfalls but did little to tamp down the moan from a woman astride a man on a red velvet settee under a pastoral oil painting.

Farther down, a man wearing a rope harness across his chest stood facing a set of French doors overlooking a flagstone terrace that spilled out and down to a garden overflowing with Roses of Sharon. It wasn't until they passed him did she glimpse a woman on the other side of the glass. She was nude except for a pair of red heels and bent over, baring her pussy to him. An ache throbbed between her own legs at her puffed-up and pink flesh.

Griffin's face showed no reaction to the scenes unfolding around them. His eyes were fixed forward on a large gothic arch that led to the Library—the one room she knew.

Play was in full swing. Loud slaps of flesh, laughter, and clinks of glass filled the air.

They passed right by the Library and every scene, every bit of action.

He pulled her down a side hall. "The other night, none of the scenes intrigued you." He stated it as a fact.

"They were interesting, just not …" Truth was they were intriguing but just not for her somehow. The various kinks—fire, water, flogging—didn't call to her. She'd do any of it if he wanted, but really, what she wanted was something she couldn't quite name yet.

They stopped before an elevator. "What?" His brows furrowed in question.

"They didn't make me desperate to try them."

His lips thinned in thought. "Hmm. Let's see what makes you desperate."

How about just looking my way?

She entered the elevator when the large door opened. "May I ask where we're going?"

"You may." He gestured for her to enter.

They left their two escorts, and the door clanged behind them.

"Are we going to a dungeon? Is that where we're going?" she whispered. She could see it. Coats of arms on concrete walls, tall knight's armor standing guard, and chains—lots and lots of chains.

A half-smile inched up on his face. "Not my aesthetic." Amusement at her assumption colored his eyes.

She'd been watching him closer each time they were together, learning his face, his different kinds of smiles—and different frowns. His sternest look came from when she jumped to conclusions.

She glanced around the ornate elevator car. "So old-fashioned." Mirrors lined the walls with intricate iron scrollwork holding them in place.

"Alexander appreciates beauty—and history." He grasped her hand, her fingers meeting something rough. He had a band-aid on his little finger. Such a small detail, but it sent her mind whirring.

Had he cut it cooking? She couldn't picture him in a kitchen. Someone would cook for him. She could do that.

Or some accident like working on his car? He would be a man who would work on his own car.

They really knew so little of each other. Yet it didn't seem to matter.

The elevator stopped with a thunk. They'd traveled two floors down and exited into a concrete hallway with plush Oriental rug runners and sconces lining the walls.

Three men in black were the only people she could see. Two stood, each flanking a different door. The third sat in a chair at the end of the hallway before a set of double doors. He rose as they approached.

Griffin nodded to the man, who drew out a set of keys and unlocked the door.

"Programming?" Griffin asked.

A curt nod from the man followed. "Yes, sir."

"Very good."

He signaled for her to step inside.

Blackness filled her sight, her heel clicks echoing against unseen surfaces as she stepped deeper within. Bits of light shone in ribbons and seemed to glide in the air. It wasn't until her eyes adjusted she understood long swaths of shiny silk hung from round hooks in the ceiling, catching the hallway light.

The room was large, about twenty feet by twenty feet, and half a dozen waterfalls of parachute silk made a forest of fabric that swayed slowly in some unseen breeze, probably from the room's air ducts.

It was oddly beautiful and stark.

"Lights."

At the sound of his voice, a glow of red rose from the floor, along the floor and ceiling edges, and from above. In the center of the room, gleaming in the red light, was a metal sawhorse, holes punched in its surface every few inches. Carabiners hung haphazardly from a few of them.

The piece was terrifying in its simplicity—and electrifying in its obvious uses.

"Your safeword has been programmed into the system. If you say it and I don't let the DM outside know we've stopped—"

"They'll storm the room?"

His lips stretched wide into a smile, and he cupped her

chin. "Something like that. And no interruptions, Colette, or you'll get a special punishment."

Special. He made everything sound delicious.

"And no, you won't like it."

Damn, he read her mind. He'd probably make her wait another week to come, which would just about kill her dead.

"Take off your clothes. And don't be neat about it. Keep the heels on."

There was no place to put them, so she shimmied out of her knit dress and let it puddle on the floor. She'd long given up wearing panties around him and opted not to even wear a bra, so after the dress hit the concrete floor, she was nude, save for her black strapped heels.

At some point, showing off her body became de rigueur. He'd had his fingers in her, eyed her bare pussy, and had his hands everywhere he could reach.

"Take a walk around the room. I want to watch you."

She trailed her hand along the nearest wall, her fingers meeting black lacquered drawer pulls and knobs. The recessed cabinets and drawers were so seamlessly part of the walls if she hadn't touched them, she might not have seen them at all.

"Silks up and open wall," he said. The whine of an engine was quickly followed by fabric rustling. Long black curtains along the other three walls retracted to the corners while the long swaths of parachute silk rose to create graceful arcs like bunting in the sky.

From every angle, her face stared back at her in the floor-to-ceiling mirrors.

His nostrils flared in his reflection. "I will see every

inch of you now."

Such a promise that there would be something to see—so captivating that he'd want to see all of her—caused a ripple of fear and anticipation. Right then, she wondered if her limits list was complete enough.

"Come here."

She teetered to where he stood by the sawhorse.

"Lay yourself over it ... slowly."

She made quite a show of draping herself over the padded top, widening her legs, and letting the cold seep into her. It raised gooseflesh the second it touched her skin.

Shoe scuffs along the concrete floor sounded behind her. His large palm circled her neck and tipped her chin up so she once more confronted her reflection.

"Look at yourself. See how flushed your skin is, how your mouth is slack, how your muscles quiver a little. You're already imagining what I can do to you in this position, aren't you?"

"Yes, Sir." More like hell, yes.

He tightened the grip on her throat. "It makes me hungry for you. To see such lust and longing this early."

Her eyes darted to his, shining at her in the mirror. Dark, charcoal, dancing with life. Griffin was the most "alive" person she'd ever met.

He pushed her head back down. Every shoe scrape, every bit of movement echoed loudly in her ears.

He roughly kicked her legs open more and secured them with silky cords to the metal frame. Her arms were next. Those he tethered to the floor with more silk rope connected to rings mounted in the concrete. It made her wish she'd studied the ceiling more, given how many secrets the walls had held.

His hands then toured her body, first to cup her breasts hanging heavy, nipples hard peaks. Then to her waist, where he spanned both palms to move down to her hips. His fingers then circled her thighs before gliding up to her ass. His fingers dug into her flesh and forced her cheeks apart.

Oh, God. She clenched out of instinct. He was seeing her most vulnerable parts—dirty, raw, and primal.

With the lightest touch of a fingertip, he traced her asshole in small circles. "Such beautiful options for someone."

Her breaths came shallow, and she couldn't seem to stop clenching her butt as he continued to touch her lazily in places no one had ever touched. He murmured a deep rumble as her thighs quaked.

A wet warmth touched right there, and she gasped. His tongue probed her tight back hole, and she whimpered. So dirty, so sweet.

One of his knees creaked as he rose to stand. He wound his hand in her hair, creating a ponytail, and gave a gentle pull so her head lifted. Just on the side of pain but not.

Scratchy cotton fabric touched her back. He was leaning over her. "Your responses are exquisite—and they please me." His hot breath ran over her neck.

A long sigh left her mouth, and she had to quickly swallow or drool.

"You didn't think I saw you back then, did you?"

Back then meant in his classroom. She knew it without even having to ask. "No." They were developing a kind of shorthand already.

"I saw everything. The way you pushed your hair off your neck on one side. How you buried your hands between your legs and squeezed them together hard when I called on you. Made me wonder what secrets you tucked between those pretty little thighs."

"Wanting." The honesty of the word shocked even her as it tumbled from her lips. She had wanted him from the second she saw him—as did everyone else. He called that up in everyone who encountered him—even men. She'd seen it in his classroom.

He chuckled low. "I will see you grow that wanting tonight, won't I?"

She rolled her lips between her teeth, worried she'd let out a bleat otherwise. "Mmmhhm,"

He let go of her hair, her scalp smarting a bit, and circled to her front.

Her vision filled with the concrete floor, and her hands curled around the two metal rings holding her bindings so her arms were outstretched.

His hardness pushed into her ass cheeks from behind, not entering but teasing her. A thought occurred. He hadn't let her ever touch him. She'd like to do more than touch—if he'd let her.

"Are you wondering what I'm going to do?"

"Yes." She nearly breathed the word. If he wanted to fuck her in the ass—which she'd never done—tonight, she'd let him.

A loud smack against her flesh answered.

"Yes, Sir."

He smacked her ass again and again, working one cheek, then the other, until her flesh had to be blossoming bruises. No warm-up, just a full-on spanking—brutal and sudden. Tiny puffs of air left her lips at each blow. For every sting of pain, pleasure arose—a need she couldn't explain.

Within minutes, her hips began to arch and press into the sawhorse, almost like she wanted to fuck it, and her skin slicked with perspiration. Whatever he planned to do, if it involved putting her on the edge and keeping her there for a while, she was already there.

A wisp of a touch drew up her spine. Something red flashed in the mirror. A long feather? Where he got it from, she'd never know. She kept her gaze on him as he stared at her ass. He stared so long that her nipples hung painfully in the air, raw peaks of need.

"As I said. Beautiful." His eyes glanced up and stared at hers in the mirror. "You thought I'd take you down here, perhaps bind you, whip you, fuck you …"

"Yes," the word escaped her throat in a long sigh. In the mirror, she could see she wasn't the only one. Gratitude that his cock was pushing against his zipper soothed her. And she so wanted to free it.

"Would you let me do this to you all night?" He ground out the words as he trailed the feather up her leg.

"Yes, Sir."

He moved the feather lightly, over her back, down her thighs. Blood raised in her skin, and her forearms grew impossibly redder in the light. Then he moved between her legs. He ran the maddening feather back and forth between her folds—a bare whisper.

Her blood raced, and her legs began to twitch as her pussy demanded attention. Instead, he worked the plume over her clit—too soft, too light—until her thighs banged against the sawhorse in irritation.

He chuckled. "Someone's ticklish."

"Not," she spat.

"Someone isn't appreciative of my attention." That maddening stroke of the feather moved up her inner thigh.

"I am. Thank you, Sir."

Another long stroke through her folds. "You'll take what I give you."

"Yes … Sir." She shuddered hard as he ran the feather along her spine, around her neck, to her cheek. "I can take anything … for you. You can … have me."

"Say the words, Colette."

"Fuck me." She didn't talk like that—ever.

"I don't fuck anyone who doesn't belong to me."

The air left the room. He wasn't going to give himself to her? He couldn't have put up such walls already. What had she done? Or not done?

The feather returned its slow trail up her inner thigh, across her crotch, and down her other inner thigh for longer than she thought she could take.

When he finally dropped it to the ground, landing quickly now that it was soaked with her juices, he pressed his torso into her back. His cock pressed against her, and the mere thought she'd never get to really feel him? He couldn't have meant that.

"What's going on in that pretty little head of yours?"

"More. Please, Sir, more." *Of you. Of all of you.*

He resumed spanking her until she was arching her ass up into the air, begging for more. More of him. She needed to be breached.

"What will I do with you, little Colette? So eager for more."

Yes.

He'd played with her—brought up a deeper desire in her than she thought possible—save one. He hadn't given himself to her—thrust inside her and taken his own pleasure.

I don't fuck anyone who doesn't belong to me. But why not? How could he not see the truth? She belonged there with him.

Perhaps because he didn't want her in that way. He said he liked giving orders—and she took them. Maybe that was all he needed.

But then his fingers were inside her, and she was riding a release that made her yank on her bindings so hard that the skin touching them had to be raw.

Chapter Six

Griffin yanked on the silk cords constraining her legs. She didn't move to get up—not until he told her to.

He freed her arms with equal speed.

He eased her up slowly, letting the blood rush through her limbs and resettle. She grew dizzy, so dizzy she couldn't sense what was up and down. The cold mirror touched her back, which helped raise her awareness.

His dark eyes glittered like obsidian, and his hair cast a purplish hue in the red light. He was so beautiful.

He cupped her cheek and gazed deeply into her eyes. He then gave her a bruising kiss.

His tongue explored every part of her mouth as he held her jaw firmly with both hands. Her hips instinctively reached for him, searching out other parts of his body.

He broke his kiss and stared down at her. "You have a hungry mouth," he rasped.

She nodded. Cold air, nerves dancing underneath her skin, her pussy feeling so empty. But most of all, after his tongue had worked her over so thoroughly, she wanted to fall to her knees and have her mouth filled with his cock.

She glanced down at that bulge, and her fingers reached out.

He grasped her wrist. "Did I say you could do that?"

She gave a tight shake of her head, which cleared the rest of her vision.

His hand fisted her hair, and he pushed her hard to her knees. One of her heels slipped off. Her hands reached out to grasp his thighs to steady herself.

"Since you're so eager …" His voice was rough, hard.

A small, rough carpet was at his feet. It burned the skin of her kneecaps as she shifted.

"Hands behind your back. Box them."

She did what he asked, and the clank of his belt buckle was quickly followed by the lowering of his zipper.

He drew himself out and showed himself to her—hard, thick, all smooth, red skin, and a wide, flared tip. A vein throbbed along the side. It was hard and so much thicker than she'd believed. The deep crimson looked painful, and she wanted to ease it.

"Only your mouth." He wound her hair tighter in his fist.

She had so little practice at taking a man this way— her other attempts clumsy under sheets in the dark. But she wanted to try with him, be good for him.

She leaned forward and ran her tongue around the tip, tasting him.

A long breath left his body, urging her. That was all she needed to hear. Her body went full five-alarm fire, all molten heat threatening to burn away any sliver of fear. She could handle it. She would, for him.

She repeated the action and then needed more. She let the ridges and swells ride over the flat of her tongue.

She did it again and again, each time wetting him further.

His breath above her grew ragged. She ran the tip of her tongue around his tip and then stabbed the little hole. Both of his hands threaded through her hair.

She took more of him; her lips stretched wide as he filled her. She pulled out and then drew him in yet another millimeter. The next time she pulled out, he sucked in a long breath.

His hips pitched forward, holding her head in place as he forced himself deep.

It took every ounce of control to keep her arms boxed behind her as she choked. Just when little black spots formed in her eyes, he yanked her head up, and she gasped. She took in big lungfuls of air, her eyes blinking with sticky tears. Her mascara had to be running down her cheeks.

He forced her to look up at him. He didn't loosen his fist one bit, but he stared down at her, questioning. He was checking on her. But more than that, he was showing her who he really was—brutal and the opposite of a feather, so much more than a spanking. He was the full spectrum. And did she want to continue?

She could call *Dante*. But she didn't want him to stop.

Her legs were rubbing against one another, squirming

with impatience and desire. She wanted him to force her again.

Her mouth reached for him again, but he stopped her. "Whenever someone does this to you ... remember, you have a choice."

She shook her head. She had no words, but someone? There were no other *someones*. Her eyes filled with Griffin, and her mouth tasted of his cock. There would never be another.

For six years, she'd dreamed of doing that with him. Years of never believing she would. Years of longing for someone she had no words for.

A lone tear escaped down her cheek.

"What is that tear for?" he rasped.

"You said someone."

"Yes, you're just at the beginning of your journey."

"No. I've arrived." She couldn't imagine being without him now. She would never get enough of this man. Not ever.

His eyes narrowed slightly as if he didn't believe her.

She made a showing of licking her lips. A long swipe of her tongue along her bottom lip and then her top lip. "Please, Sir." He said she'd beg for more.

His eyes glinted with pleasure—perhaps not because of her answer, but because he was, at that moment, fully himself. In control. Satisfied. With someone who wanted him. What a funny thought that he would need reassurance.

The mere thought she could be of service to him, make him feel wanted, was enough for her pussy to thrum with impossible need.

His cock breached her lips again, that time harder and

with more force. She sucked air in through her nose and felt the long, forceful glide of him.

"Relax."

She pictured her throat opening, taking him in, the pleasure he might feel from the warmth and slickness of her tongue. He moved out slowly, and another long inhale filled her lungs. The next time he pushed in, he went even farther, the tip of his cock hitting the back of her throat.

Choking, she willed her arms to stay behind her. Each time he went in a little farther, deeper.

Her tears streamed freely, and her nose ran. Noisy breaths in and out.

His hand never left his fist hold. But the fingers of his other hand were under her chin, tipping her head back so she could take even more of him, the tips of them caressing her cheek, and he was murmuring something. Encouragement.

"Yes, little Colette. You've got this. Now, all of me." With one more thrust, he went even farther than before.

Her throat closed around his cock, and new tears escaped her eyes. He groaned loudly, spurring her courage. She sucked her cheeks in, feeling all of him.

That was when he started fucking her mouth in earnest. Each time, he pulled nearly all the way out so she could draw in air, then he'd push back in.

She swallowed, and she tried so hard to keep her eyes open to watch the veins in his throat grow more pronounced, his jaw tense, and him seething between his teeth.

He was thrusting then, and they worked up a rhythm. Breath. Thrust. Breath. Thrust.

Her neck ached, her knees were numb, and she was

nothing but a receptacle for his cock. He was loving it, and she grew elated that she might be giving him such pleasure. She could come just from how he held her there … possessive and in control.

Only she wouldn't dare. She wouldn't break the sacred moment where she became a service vehicle; him the one with the need.

The reversal of roles was so sharp—at first, he, the master, and she, the slave. Now? She was the one who had what he needed. Him at the mercy of it. The power was intoxicating.

He held himself deep inside her finally, and she swallowed a few times as he emptied himself into her.

When he pulled out, a rush of adrenaline filled her body as she sucked in air. Her hands fell to the floor as she breathed hard. His hand was still in her hair.

Then he kneeled and wiped her cheeks, smearing mascara and lipstick on her skin. He pushed her gently to her side and left her on the cool concrete. "Stay there."

Oh, maybe there would be more. Her cunt was ready— so ready for anything he wanted—as her desire dripped down her thighs and to the floor.

He strode to one wall and pushed on it. A drawer slid out. So many secrets at Accendos.

He returned with a steaming washcloth. He eased her to sitting against him and immediately began to swipe the cloth across her mouth, under her eyes, and down her neck. "You did well … little Colette."

Gentle kisses against her temple. Such care. She wanted to curl into his body, never leave. "Thank you, Sir."

"Do you have questions? You have permission to ask me anything."

His return to business stilled her heart.

His hand rested on her cheek, the little band-aid flashing in her vision as he moved the washcloth down her arms.

"What did you do to your finger?" The words just came out.

Another flash of surprise crossed his face. "Opening a package. One of those god-awful plastic molds."

She placed her hand over his and turned her face so she could press a small kiss where the band-aid covered. "I wish I could have taken the cut for you."

"Ah, but that's my job."

"I want a job."

"Tired of translations so soon in your career?" He chuckled and stood, drawing her up with him. "Let's go upstairs and get you cleaned up more."

She pulled at his shirt lapels. "I don't want to leave. Next week—"

"I have to go out of town."

Her heart sank. No, she nearly died. A hole began to form in her chest from the mere thought of not seeing him, touching him.

"I'll be back on Friday," he said.

"I'll be here."

He cupped her chin. "So, you wish to continue."

"I want nothing more."

"Then you'll do something while I'm gone."

"Yes."

He chuckled again. "Always so eager. You will think of

what you want, really want, moving forward."

"I'd say yes to anything."

A low rumble vibrated against her torso as he drew her closer. "You say that now." He brushed the hair from her face. "But you'll do this for me. And put it in writing."

"I will, Sir." She couldn't puzzle out what words to use right then. Her mind was fuzzy, and she had to hang onto his arm to steady herself as he led her to where her dress lay puddled on the floor.

She'd abandoned it so long ago, right? Time had slipped.

After helping her get her dress back on, he led her out. The men in black, still standing guard, stood as they passed. Then she found herself in a ladies' room with a woman named Carrie. She said her name three times as if she knew it would be futile for Colette to remember anything right then.

With warm hands and an even warmer smile, she urged Colette to empty her bladder, sip some water, and use a moist towelette over her neck, wrists, and anywhere else she still felt sticky. She even offered her different clothes, but Colette wouldn't change.

She wasn't ready to let go of the memories the dress held, just a few minutes ago haphazardly abandoned on a concrete floor—the first night Griffin allowed her to touch him.

At her apartment door, he placed a kiss on her forehead. He then reached into his jacket pocket and pulled out a small, leather-bound journal.

"Write down what you want." He held it out to her. "When I return from London on Friday, we'll discuss it."

Her fingers curled around the smooth leather spine and nodded as she held it close to her breast.

When she closed her apartment door, she slunk to the floor, the beautiful journal under her fingers. She brought it up to her nose and inhaled. It smelled like lavender and him.

How would she go a week without seeing him?

Her phone buzzed in her hand. She hadn't even recalled holding it.

<<Friday. Noon. My office. Bring the journal with something in it.>>

How about her heart?

Chapter Seven

Seven days. They passed as slowly as the gray, fat clouds overhead—heavy and with no sense of the urgency of her situation.

The first day away from him—Saturday—her high from the trip to Accendos lifted. His kiss at her door the night before still burned on her forehead, but her belly was hollow, and her mind just wouldn't clear. He called her in the late morning, but his voice sounded so distant on the phone, saying he was catching his plane. That his communication would be spotty, but she should contact him anytime, day or night.

His offer heartened her, but then Sunday, her mind fog cleared. The clarity only sharpened the words she couldn't stop thinking.

You are just at the beginning of your journey.
Whenever someone does this to you.

She called Charlotte, who reassured her the mind spins

were normal and urged her to text Griffin. She did, and he answered with short, curt answers. *Yes. No. You're going to be okay.* It was a pale substitute for hearing his voice, but apparently, his conference kept him going all day and night.

If that was what was going on at all. A strange paranoia settled over her. Charlotte said that was normal, too, though, "…no two situations are the same. You just feel what you feel."

She didn't want to appear needy, unable to handle what they'd done. So she didn't call him. She just dealt with it.

But then, a few days later, she got a longer text. *Beautiful, how are you? Feeling all right? Call me if you need me.* She did.

"I miss you," she blurted out as soon as he answered.

"I miss you, too, beautiful. Being thinking of me?"

He had to ask? "Always."

"Same." An odd lilt had colored his voice as if he didn't believe it himself. "How are you, Colette?"

She loved hearing her name on his lips. "I'm okay. How's the conference?"

"Boring. What did you do today?" Fabric rustled like he was shifting.

"Translated a blog post on the five rarest bee species. Exciting stuff."

He laughed, a sound she hadn't heard often. Deep, rumbling that made her think of his broad chest and strength.

"I like hearing you laugh," she said.

"Hmmm. Not many people make me do it."

"Oh, I'm sorry I—"

"Colette," he said gently. "I enjoy you when you're

relaxed."

She couldn't help it. She snorted. "Oh? I thought the opposite."

"Making you relaxed and happy is one of my greatest joys."

She swallowed, and her desire, just barely banked, flamed to life. "I want to make you happy, too."

"You do."

She rolled to her side, nestled deeper into her pillow. "I'm glad."

"Tell me, other than what we've done together, what do you enjoy doing? What relaxes you?"

"Do? Um. I read. And …" She didn't want to say it. He might think her hobby silly.

"And?" he urged.

Her belly fluttered at his interest. Oh, what the hell. "I love botanical gardens. I mean, I like to discover a new one or park every week. It's kind of a … thing I do." Though not lately, because one tall, dark-haired man consumed her every waking moment. "It's how I met Charlotte, actually. At Bishop's Garden. Do you know it?"

"I do. It's lovely. Rare. Have you seen Accendos' gardens yet?"

"No, though I hear they're spectacular." Alexander Rockingham had apparently created an outdoor oasis at his home-turned-club. She'd heard it was the envy of all in Washington, DC—at least those who knew about it. Few photographs existed.

"It is," he said. "Picture wide flagstones that weave a path through tall boxwoods and trees surrounded by roses, hibiscus, lilies … So many flower species." His voice got a little dreamy. She didn't expect him to be such a poet—and not about flowers. It warmed her that he'd appreciate something she also loved.

"I heard he has more than fifty Black Baccara red rose bushes."

"Yes. I'll take you."

"I'd love that." She'd love anything where he was involved, but most of all, something about making plans with him gave her hope.

"His gardens hold quite a few secrets."

Her lips stretched into a smile. "Like what?"

"It wouldn't be a secret if I told you." A tease colored his voice. "The place needs to be seen, experienced."

"And you'll take me, really?" She almost couldn't believe it, and she silently prayed her insecurities didn't come through in her voice.

"Of course. Much of it should be in bloom right now."

Her heart did a little happy dance. "Thank you. The gardens sound a bit wild but still elegant."

"Like you. But you're more beautiful."

Her breath hitched, and she was momentarily stunned. He'd called her beautiful before, but something felt different. Perhaps it was the conversation—the fact that they were talking about things that didn't involve spanking or bondage. Or maybe she was like a starving rabbit needing a carrot, and he'd given it to her with his attention, admiration. Still, the knot she'd been carrying around in her shoulders instantly eased.

"What do you like to do? I mean, to relax?" she asked.

"What we've been doing. How's the journal coming?"

He asked the one question she dreaded. Mood broken, she swallowed thickly. She couldn't bear to disappoint him, so she lied. "Good."

"I like hearing that."

Her stomach roiled a little. She'd have to confess her lie if she didn't get off the stick about the journal—something she thought would be easy to fill out. Instead, it sat empty, taunting her every time she glanced at it on her nightstand.

"Whatever you wrote interests me deeply, Colette."

Two emotions warred inside her over his statement. She wanted his attention—all of it. But his *interest* wasn't enough.

She yawned before she could stop herself, and he caught it.

"I've kept you long enough," he said.

Her breath stalled. She knew what he meant. Time to go to sleep, but they landed like he was cutting her loose.

"Have a good night," she managed to get out.

"I'll see you soon."

And then he was gone, and she didn't hear from him for the next two days. Maybe he knew she'd lied? Maybe he was cutting her loose? Why was her imagination trying to kill her? She had to get a grip.

Friday morning dawned clear and bright, but her mood remained dark. The journal remained blank, though she'd tried every day to fill it with something—anything. She was sure he didn't mean for her to write about field trips to Alexander's gardens. Or did he?

Her brain was mush. Everything she thought of felt …

wrong. Or, rather, *incomplete*. Or worse, it might not be what he wished for.

Did he like to play with ropes? Floggers? Some of the scary-looking furniture she'd seen in Club Accendos' Library?

Did he want to see her in a cat costume? Dress as a French maid? Don bunny ears and hop around like the lunatic she was beginning to grow into?

The truth was, what she wanted might be more than he'd be willing to give, and she couldn't bear the thought of hearing him turn her down. She wanted more of their Wednesday night conversation, something normal and hopeful. Or how close it made her feel to him anyway.

She needed help, so she begged Charlotte to meet her for coffee Friday morning.

"What are you obsessing about?" Charlotte smiled at her over her coffee cup.

"I haven't heard from him in two days."

"But you're meeting him today, and he probably spent all day yesterday traveling. Then there's jet lag …" Charlotte sipped her coffee.

Her friend was trying to make her feel better.

Charlotte's cup clinked to the saucer. "What time do you see him?"

"In four hours. In his office."

"Oh, his office." Charlotte's smile disappeared.

"What does it mean?"

She eyed the small journal by her coffee. "He probably wants to go over that. Still don't know what to put in there? What do you want?"

"Oh, I know what I want." Or who. "I just don't know how to phrase it." Which was ridiculous, given her entire job was working with words.

"It's not always easy to articulate it. But knowing you, you're seeking the perfect words."

She was. There were things he could show her she didn't even realize she'd want. She was sure of it.

Charlotte sighed. "Look, my best advice is just to write the bottom line. What is the one thing you two could do together you can't live without? Start there."

"Hmm." She chewed the inside of her cheek. She knew, but … She shook her head. "He wouldn't."

"You'd be surprised." Charlotte reached around and grabbed her coat off the back of the chair. "I've got to get to work. We're installing an outdoor classroom at St. Mary's next week, and the landscaping crew has a million questions … still." She rolled her eyes.

Colette had always known Charlotte to be so reserved. To hear her talk with such confidence heartened her. Perhaps that was what happened when you found yourself in your perfect place?

That was it. She finally admitted the truth to herself. There was only one thing she wanted: her perfect place.

She rose with Charlotte. "Thank you." She leaned over and gave her a quick hug. "I think I've got it now."

~~~~

Colette rapped on his office door at 11:59, according to her phone. There was no answer, though she heard his rumbly voice inside. Was he with someone?

She pressed her ear to the glass, and it fell away under

her cheek. She snapped upright. "Sorry, Sir."

His smile warmed her from head to foot. "Punctual as ever, Miss Martin."

It was the first time he'd used her last name. The formality niggled at her.

She moved inside and found no one. He must have been on the phone. "How are you?" she asked quickly. "How was the rest of your trip?"

"Fruitful." He circled to the back of his desk and sat in his chair, gesturing for her to take the seat opposite of him. "How are you?" He arched an eyebrow.

The air was stifling with the small talk. "I'm good. I …"

"Yes?"

Missed you. Thought about you. Needed you. "Thank you for seeing me." She set the journal on his desk and returned her hands to her lap. "I brought it." She lowered her lashes.

His chair creaked as he shifted. "Very good."

"It's not exactly a 'want to do stuff' list, but …"

"It's what you want." He nodded. "Read it to me."

Read it aloud? Her eyes darted up to his face, and her lips parted.

"What's that hesitation?"

"It's just I …"

"Stand."

She rose but kept her gaze down.

"You might need some incentive. Lean over the desk." He opened his top drawer.

The sound was familiar. Had it only been twenty-one days ago when he brought out three items, displayed them for her, and made her choose one?

She bent at her waist and laid herself across the papers scattered on his desk surface. The smell of the leather journal near her face comforted her. She would never take in that scent again without thinking of him. But then, everything had become about him so quickly.

Her body relaxed. If you'd asked her a few weeks ago if this position would have been comfortable, she'd have believed she lost her mind. Now, it seemed to be the most natural thing in the world.

When his hand clasped the back of her neck, a long sigh escaped from her lips.

"I missed you," she breathed. It was so strange how the truth just came out when she was in his presence, but especially when he was touching her.

As he rounded his desk, he let his hand trail from her neck, down her spine, to just above the crack of her ass. She quivered a little at the warmth.

He laughed. "Were you a good girl while I was gone?"

Was she? She hadn't played with herself, gotten off at all. But then, it never occurred to her to do such a thing. He had said her orgasms belonged to him, and somehow, it just became a way of life.

How quickly her life had changed.

Fabric brushed against her ass as he lifted her skirt.

"I like this skirt. The mix of dark and sweet."

"I bought it for you." On Thursday, when she was still counting down the hours to Friday, she'd seen it in the window of a little shop in Georgetown. It was a cheap skirt. Black cotton with a pattern of tiny roses scattered across the hemline.

His hand palmed her ass cheek. She, of course, was bare.

That was another thing. She rarely wore panties anymore. She had to really think about it every morning before she went to work. Today, she didn't have to think at all. She was going to see Griffin. So the skirt went on, and the panties stayed off.

His fingertip lazily drew up her thigh. "I've missed these responses from you. And I look forward to seeing what you wrote in the journal."

Her body stiffened a little. Was she ready for him to see it? Courage—that was what she wanted to display, but perhaps she'd overplayed her hand with her entry.

Still, she'd done what Charlotte had said. She sat in the parking lot, took a big breath, and wrote, in big letters, eight words. That's all it took to express exactly what she wanted.

Rough trouser pants pressed to the back of her thighs. And his bulge just barely touched her above her ass cheeks.

He placed one hand along her head, and the other reached for the journal. He flipped the page open. The room went still.

Oh. God. He was reading her eight words.

She swallowed hard. She wanted to say something, but what? Sorry if it disappointed you? What would she do if he said "no"?

"I see." He held it up to her, but she didn't need to see it. "Read it."

Okay, big breath. Stop being a rabbit. "Belong to Master Griffin. Be his only someone."

He fisted her hair, and a delicious shudder ran through her. "Belong. That's a strong word."

"Yes, Sir."

"You wish to be bound to me? Mine?"

She gave the only answer she could. The only answer she was destined to give. "Yes."

"Do you know what that means?"

"I am yours and only yours. There is no one else, Sir."

"You want me to take possession forever … here." He roughly forced his hand under her chest and squeezed her breast.

She nodded.

He then moved his hand down her side, curled his fingers under one thigh, and roughly yanked it open. He thrust a finger inside her. "And here?"

She was so wet. The minute she saw his name on the door, it had started. But lying across his desk? As she had so many times? She could have returned the Sahara Desert to a garden.

"Yes, sir."

He spent long minutes driving her mad with kisses, bites, and licks up her earlobe. She swore she felt the thrum of his pulse in his neck touch hers. Was he pleased? Testing her? All she knew was that she'd give anything for him to keep going.

"And?" He kept asking her every time he moved to another part of her body.

Her answer was the same—always. "Yes, Sir. Yours."

But when he slipped his hand under her chest to just over her heart, she whimpered. "Especially there."

He'd said they'd find out what she was desperate for. It wasn't any kind of play or scene or kink. It came down to one thing—him.

His mouth claimed her neck while his hand passed over every part of her torso, the other with a firm hold of her hair. All firm, deliberate touches. She'd learned over the last two weeks how tentative other men had been. Clumsy, searching … and nothing like Griffin's moves. Hesitation wasn't in his repertoire.

He yanked her upright and held her against him. His chest was rising and falling, and within seconds, her breath matched his. She took it as a sign.

"I haven't had … someone in a very long time," he rasped in her ear.

"I never have." Sure, she'd had boyfriends, but no one who was that *special* someone. A man she'd consider being with her entire life. Now, a life without her Master couldn't be. He may reject her, but she'd always be his.

His cheek lifted against her hair. He was smiling? "No one? I find that hard to believe. You're special."

She twisted to nestle into him. He let her. His warmth and strength met her cheek. "Only when I'm with you."

"Yours is not a light offer."

He wanted time to consider? She supposed it was fair, though she might die if another second passed without knowing how he felt. She peered up at him. "I know. And if you don't want—"

Cool air replaced the warmth as he put a little space between them. His hands cupped her cheeks, stopping her words. "No. I want. I meant you giving yourself to me is a priceless treasure. I've learned you're incomparable, Colette."

"I lied about the journal." She had to get it out. "The other night, but it was the only time, and I—"

"I know." He smiled down at her and dropped his hands down to her neck. "Your voice gave it away."

She dropped her gaze. "You knew? Of course, you did. You know everything."

"No, I don't. I had no idea you wanted …"

"You?" She lifted her lashes. "It's always been you. Always will be."

"There's so much more to explore."

Her grin couldn't be contained, and he chuckled at her response.

He rested his forehead on hers. "So much."

Their stance was so intimate, sweet, that her eyes pricked. "Can we do some of it in the Accendos gardens?" She had a fantasy of a scene outdoors, and now that some invisible seal had been broken, her mind tumbled with all kinds of things she wanted to do with him—but only him.

"We can." He sucked in a long breath and rose to his full height. His hand left her, and he stepped back, smile dropping. "But first, turn around and assume the position. We start now."

She gave him a view of her back and lowered herself to the desk.

His belt buckle clanked. *Oh, God, yes, please.* Let that sound mean what she thought it meant. His hand fisted her hair, the pull on her scalp both delicious and stinging.

"Being mine means forever, Colette." Another firm tug

on her hair. "Are you ready?"

"Always ready for you, Sir."

He pushed into her, and she was lost. Lost for good. Lost to his heaven.

But she heard his voice through all the pleasure. "Then you are ..." One more thrust. "... mine."

Finally. His.

The Portrait

Chapter One

ERIC

Nothing compared to the sound of an open palm on flesh. That sharp crack, followed by a gasp or moan, always sent a shiver of pleasure up Eric's spine.

"Are you telling the truth?" Master Griffin asked the woman strapped to the spanking bench. More crying ensued. Eric had to hand it to Lina. He'd been watching the scene for the better part of an hour. She was tough.

A feminine snuffle was next. "No."

That was the first honest thing to come out of Lina's mouth all day. She'd once again refused to follow simple protocol, something she often did to get attention.

She'd paraded down the hallway and stopped before two men. One was standing on a ladder attempting to fix a sconce that had been knocked off the wall. Master Griffin had merely offered to hold the ladder. The fact that she was wholly nude wasn't lost on either of the unsuspecting men. Especially since Master Griffin found himself gripped by Lina's arms, her bare breasts on either side of his calf.

Lina often had to be reminded by Alexander himself of the rules of the game. No breaking into another's scene. No playing without her consent being witnessed. No forcing a punishment with a smart mouth. No putting another's safety at risk.

And Alexander, Club Accendos' owner, standing silently in the archway, ever watchful of the play in the Library, took his protocol seriously.

For the whole afternoon, Eric had also stood watch. Alexander stopping by to check on things wasn't unusual. Neither was how the very air changed when he entered the room, a level of seriousness draping over everyone like a blanket.

His icy blue eyes never landed on Eric. Rather, like a king surveying his kingdom, Alexander's focus remained on the people writhing, moaning, and loving one another. He looked as natural standing there watching a woman suck off two men at once as if he was merely witnessing a check-out clerk loading groceries into bags.

His acceptance of how others expressed themselves was legendary. Club Accendos had been his main focus for nearly thirty-five years, providing a safe place for people like him and the other members. At least it had been the man's seemingly sole purpose in life until Eric and Rebecca had come along. Then everything changed. The three of them had a unique bond; one Eric would protect with his life.

Every morning, Eric woke up, twisted his head on his pillow to drink in Alexander's profile on the pillow next to him, and thanked God the man existed, let alone loved him—as well as Rebecca.

It took him and Rebecca months to get Alexander to retire from his Grand Arbiter role at Accendos. In his early sixties, he deserved a break. But it only lasted eleven months. Now, he was back at his desk attacking paperwork, settling disputes, and watching over his club's members.

Eric loved Accendos, but he'd give anything to be back "out in the wild," as Rebecca so aptly put it.

Their trips together over the last year were the stuff of dreams. The three of them had visited everywhere, from the Arashiyama Bamboo Forest in Japan to Easter Island in Chile. But it was in South Africa he could have stayed forever. Just remembering what they did in their Kagga Kamma Nature Reserve room, nestled in a rock formation, got him hard. Hard as the stone had been over their heads.

But then the call came in from Sarah's two lovers, Steffan and Laurent. Things had gone south at home. Sarah, who'd been left in charge of Accendos, had moved back to her room at the club "for the time being" to "oversee the sudden interest in bending the rules and protocol." Abandoning her live-in situation with Steffan and their shared submissive Laurent was all it took for Alexander to jet them home—and go straight back to work.

Eric understood the urgency. As soon as they'd walked back through the door of Accendos last month, he could tell something was off. The air was unsettled, voices were tense in the hallways, and strangers he didn't recognize were showing up all hours of the day and night.

Sarah, who'd taken over for Alexander, had done a valiant job at trying to keep things in order. But moving back to her room at Accendos a month into her Grand Arbiter role just to ensure basic safety at Accendos? Heavy is the head that wears the crown and all that nonsense was thrown at Alexander when he confronted her. Eric knew the truth. When the cat's away, the mice will stage a coup, forgetting what drew them to Accendos to begin with: Order, safety, and privacy.

Alexander had shut the club down for an entire week, threatening to yank everyone's membership if they didn't get with the program or ensure others were. It felt damned good to hear him deliver the news at the top of his lungs in the middle of the Library. It was a reminder of the man's power.

Now, if only Alexander would direct some of that raw energy Eric's way instead of the mountain of paperwork that he'd confronted like a hungry lion.

They say all honeymoons must end, but Alexander's recent tensions and workaholic nature niggled at Eric, whose sexual standards were raised higher than he'd thought possible from the last year. It was natural for things to slow down at some point. He scrubbed his chin, annoyed at his own thanklessness.

After all, he got to sleep in the same bed as the man every night, along with Rebecca. He got to love them both. *Be* loved by them. He got more than he'd ever dreamed of.

Their frenzied lovemaking in the middle of the night

should be enough. But something was off, and it wasn't just Alexander's return to his desk. It was something he and Rebecca talked about often—how much Alexander was working and not playing, namely with them. Or rather, with Eric.

A long moan brought him back to the present. Alexander had asked him to keep watch in the Library. He had to remain focused.

Master Griffin continued to rain blows on the woman's ass as she writhed in her bonds, thick black cuffs at the wrists binding her to rings on the floor and even thicker straps across her legs and torso keeping her on the bench. How Eric wished he was in her place. If nothing else, it might get a rise out of Alexander and give him ideas. Not that he'd ever break protocol.

He glanced up again to where Alexander stood, but the man had vanished. Probably to return to his desk. Eric was almost jealous of the thing—getting to feel the man's hands more than he had lately.

Eric touched the thick platinum link bracelet around his wrist. The one Alexander had gifted him for Christmas last year. A platinum plate rimmed with black diamond baguettes that read OURS. It was meant as a reminder that Eric would always belong to him and Rebecca. He touched it often, wanting the message to sink in.

His gaze drifted to a man strapped to the tall Library ladder, a makeshift St. Andrew's Cross. Sharp cracks of leather against flesh made him shiver once more. Alexander had once tied him to that ladder and worked him over with an evil stick so hard he'd orbited the planet a dozen times in subspace. It was their first CNC scene. Consenting to non-consent wasn't anything he'd done before. But with Alexander? He trusted the man with his life.

His mind drifted back to another scene, their first one in the dungeon below them. Rebecca had disappeared for a week, and Alexander's barely-contained grief needed an outlet. He'd offered himself. Alexander took it—with a vengeance.

Jesus, Eric's cock now pulsed against his zipper. He needed to stop thinking about the past.

"Hey, man." Tony's voice made Eric nearly jump out of his shoes. "Lina at it again?"

He stretched his neck as if that would make any more room in his pants. "When is she not?"

"Truth. Go ahead. I got this until Marcus arrives."

He slapped the guy on the back. "Thanks. I was about to unload if I had to spend another second watching."

Tony chuckled. "Alexander's in his office."

Was Eric's desperation for the man that evident? Of course, it was. Eric inched his chin up and headed out.

Alexander's office was on the second floor. Its large glass windows overlooked the spectacular gardens in the back of the house. It was winter, and nothing but stark, bare trees waved at him in the blustery cold when he entered. Clarisse, Alexander's assistant, knew Eric and Rebecca had carte blanche to enter at will.

Rebecca was inside, her red hair shining in the warm light from the lamps scattered throughout the large office. She perched on one of the grand leather chairs by his desk, laughing. Alexander was leaning back in his large executive chair, with his fingers steepled together and his icy blue eyes affixed to her.

Eric's heart did what it always did at seeing them. Danced like a Lipizzaner stallion.

He leaned against the door jamb. "Attempting a rescue mission, Rebecca?" She'd been valiantly trying to get him up from behind that monstrosity of a desk as much as Eric had.

Alexander glanced up and gestured for him to come in. "Thought you were downstairs."

"And I thought you were retired." Alexander didn't seem to notice his snarky comment, or he chose to ignore it. Thirty days ago, before they'd returned, his tone would have been addressed with a flogger, riding crop, or worse. His heart panged, missing that version of Alexander.

Eric pushed off and strode forward, "Tony's downstairs."

"Ah." Alexander's chair creaked as it thunked upright. "And this is me retired, at least while Sarah is still on her vacation, and order is restored for good."

Rebecca stood, rounded the desk and his chair, and placed her hands on his shoulder. Her low-cut T-shirt gave Eric a spectacular view of the crease between her breasts while her yoga pants hugged the curve of her ass. She began to rub Alexander's shoulders.

Alexander let out a sigh at the touch. The urge to drop to his knees, crawl over, and service the man between the legs rose so hard and fast that Eric had to clear his throat.

He scrubbed his chin, more to distract himself than anything else. Alexander needed to be in control at all times. The surest way to *not* get the man's attention was to forget that one fact.

"I'm shocked Sarah went," Rebecca said. Eric was, too.

Alexander chuckled. "Kicking and screaming, but Steffan has a way with her like no other. Laurent, too."

Sarah was lucky to have two men—one Dominant, one Submissive. Eric wouldn't have been surprised if Steffan, a Dominant by nature, hadn't tied her up and hauled her away on his shoulder to make her take some time off. He'd have paid good money to see it, actually. Maybe it'd give Alexander ideas.

Man, he needed to get handled by the man, and soon.

Rebecca gave a delicate sigh as she continued to work on Alexander's shoulders, inching her fingers closer to his chest. "Laurent's not unlike Eric, is he?" She smiled up at him. "Irresistible."

Eric swallowed down a chuff. "Oh, right, so irresistible," he still gritted out.

Alexander's eyes locked on him, and Eric hated himself for assessing the man's face for a sign that he'd agreed with Rebecca. Over a year of being loved by Alexander, and still, he evaluated every tone of voice, every twitch in his jaw like a puppy circling his owner's legs, begging for a pat on the head.

Alexander murmured. "Eric and Laurent do both have a way with people—mostly charming the pants off anything that wears pants. Or dresses. Or burlap bags if the occasion presents itself."

Only he didn't want to charm the pants off anyone other than the present company. Still, the level of pleasure Eric received from Alexander's agreement was ridiculous.

The man continued to stare at him. "Especially when he's in any of my favorite positions. On his knees. Bound. Strapped to something immovable."

Ah, maybe the gods listened? Eric inched forward more. "Whatever you'd like. Whenever you'd like." Eric was more switch than submissive, but for Alexander, he was anything required. Especially right then. He couldn't expect to watch all that play in the Library and not get immediate ideas, especially now and after so long.

Then again, sadists enjoyed the giving and taking away, hurting and kissing to make it better—eventually.

Alexander grabbed Rebecca's hand and pulled her from behind him. "Sit on the desk. Let me see you."

She perched herself in front of him. "You have much more work to do, Alexander?"

"Always."

She began to swing her legs back and forth like a little girl perched on her daddy's desk. "Wouldn't you rather be back in South Africa?"

"Ah, so this conversation again." He sliced his gaze to Eric, then back to Rebecca again.

She gave him a wry smile. "It's just …" She moved to ease herself off the desk but stopped when he tsked.

"Did I say to leave your position? Slip those leggings off. Panties, too. Eric, door."

Eric swallowed down a smile that attempted to rise. *Thank fuck.* He clicked shut Alexander's massive office door and ran his fingers down the deep filigree cuts in the wood before turning as if to remind himself he was there. And with any luck about to get down and dirty with the two people he loved most in the world.

Then again, Eric had learned never to assume what the man had planned.

Alexander grasped the back of her knees and yanked her closer. "Lean back. Eric needs to see you better."

"Require my assistance?" He moved to stand nearer to him and Rebecca.

Alexander glanced up at him, his icy blue eyes deliciously assessing him. "You are. Just by being here."

Ah, so he was going to watch? Delayed gratification was often something he had to endure with Alexander, but even a saint could run out of patience.

"Lean back. Hands on the desk behind you." As Alexander leaned back in his chair again, a creak broke the silence. "Now, tell me specifically what you two want. And don't deny it. You do want something."

Rebecca's face stilled. "I wasn't thinking of anything specific."

Sure, she wasn't. He loved Rebecca with every part of his heart, but he knew her. She loved to tease.

"Are you sure?" Alexander leaned forward and buried his index finger inside her. She gasped and whimpered but amazingly didn't move her hands.

His fingers moved ever so slightly, earning another sharp intake of air from her. "What. Do. You. Want?"

"Whatever you want." A long groan left her throat.

Eric almost let all the things he'd willingly beg for at that moment spill from his mouth, but he held it all back. The question wasn't aimed at him.

Alexander inserted a third finger. "I could watch you

in this position all day. In fact, I'd like to hang a portrait of your nude body over my mantle." His eyes sliced to an empty spot on the wall. "Legs open, inviting me in."

She smiled—a slow inching up of her lips that signaled perhaps she could also picture such a thing. Eric could see it, too. No face. Just her knees, wide, with all her pink flesh glistening … Eric's zipper could bust open from the mere mental picture. Two years ago, if you'd told him he'd have a thing for two people at once, he'd have asked the person what drug they were on. Now, loving these two people, needing them, was as natural as breathing.

Alexander quickened his fingers. "You'd do that for me, wouldn't you?"

She blinked and sucked in a long breath. She was close. "What?"

"Sit for a painter. Let him paint you. Like this."

Her eyes widened, and she nodded. "Whatever you wish."

He withdrew his finger, and a protesting whine left her throat.

So Alexander would continue to keep them on edge a little longer. Patience gone, Eric moved closer and let his thighs hit the desk. "Doesn't sound like many wishes are being granted."

Alexander didn't look up at him, but a tell-tale twitch in his jaw spoke for him. Eric was in so much trouble. He wasn't sorry. What he was, was out of options.

Alexander rose. "Let's go, all three of us. Finish this elsewhere."

"That means we'll—"

"That means I'll consider whatever you two have yet to ask me for."

Eric would be happy to spell it out for him—preferably with his tongue.

Chapter Two

ERIC

Alexander was a dick. Not that Eric would ever say such a thing to his face—at least not willingly. Not if he wanted to keep his balls attached to his person. Plus, he also was a dick Eric loved.

Eric struggled against the thick black cords banding his arms behind his back. His knees chaffed anew as he attempted to balance himself. The key word was "attempt." Tony was driving and yet another dick, given how he was swinging through Capital Beltway traffic—likely on purpose, knowing Eric was bound and struggling to stay upright before Alexander in the back of the limo.

Alexander's gaze moved to Eric, giving him a direct view of his ice-blue eyes. They nearly pierced his soul. "Eric, watch her, not me." The man's smooth voice did little to soothe the aching flagpole between Eric's legs.

Eric obeyed and shifted his focus to Rebecca, whose creamy, bare ass faced him. The smattering of freckles across her lower back taunted him as her head bobbed up and down, doing exactly what *Eric* wanted to be doing. *Should* be doing.

The floor underneath him shifted, and Eric nearly pitched over—again.

Alexander chuckled and shifted in his seat, probably to shove himself farther down Rebecca's throat. "I rather enjoy your reaction to her. What she's doing right now." His eyes drifted down to Eric's cock—painful and bobbing with every pothole Tony had to be aiming for at that point.

Eric lifted his gaze to Alexander. "What can I do for you?"

"You're doing it. Drinking this whole scene in. Desiring me—and Rebecca."

It was impossible for him to be any other way. That powerful man had chosen him—allowed him into his world and his heart. Just lately, not inside him.

Alexander sat back in the seat and put his hand on her head to still her movements. "Rebecca, love, take a breather. Sit up here next to me."

Rebecca sat back on her heels and then scrambled to sit beside him. The little vixen spread her legs wide, giving Eric a load of both her goods *and* Alexander's, which still stood at attention. A part of the man, Eric realized, he probably wouldn't get to touch for a while.

Alexander's hand drifted over Rebecca's thigh, and his fingers played with her until her head fell back, and she panted. "Eric, I'm seriously considering having Rebecca's portrait done now. I want your expert opinion."

"On?"

"The artist." His lips inched up into a half smile. "And the angle."

What the devil was he talking about? "She's perfect at every angle." He didn't hide his crankiness. Maybe he'd earn a punishment. Anything to end this torture of being shut out of the action.

Alexander's fingers quickened, and Rebecca's eyes lighted on him, mascara-stained cheeks glistening in the light coming through the tinted glass.

"Yes, but I think this pose, with her legs spread and her head thrown back, might be what I'm seeking. Who do you know who could capture such beauty?"

The vixen chewed on her bottom lip and groaned. She fought not to come. "Please," she choked out.

"No." Alexander's middle finger continued to draw lazy circles between her legs.

They were both at Alexander's mercy. Always had been. And he doled out mercy like a narcotic—carefully measured and infrequent.

Alexander's hands stilled. "Keep them open, Rebecca."

She panted, her stormy gray eyes fixed on Alexander. A gentle affection flickered in the ice blue of his for a second.

He turned to Eric. "You need to get closer, Eric. To really give me your fine art opinion."

He inched closer as best he could, given his arms were unavailable. When the limo lurched, Alexander's hand shot out. His fingers wrapped around Eric's bicep, steadying him. Their gaze locked for one brief second, enough for the intoxicating spell of belonging to him to gush through his veins like an opioid.

"Sit back." Alexander released his hold, and Eric resettled onto his ankles. The man encircled him in a kind of awkward hug but soon realized Alexander was merely reaching to untie his bindings.

"I want you"—a yank of the cord released tension in his shoulders—"to tell me"—the cords slithered against his skin as the knots were undone—"how you would paint Rebecca like this."

The cords fell to the floor, and Eric massaged his hands, bringing the blood flow back to the surface. Alexander always did bind him tight, as if Eric might get away. Fat chance.

"No painting could adequately depict Rebecca." He'd know, having handled many estate sales with the finest private collections available. Van Goghs. Rembrandts. Warhols. "She's more than a moment in time."

Alexander's eyes danced, and a fresh course of gratitude flowed through his veins—that time because he'd pleased the man with his answer. Eric was so easy, wasn't he? From gratitude to irritation back to gratitude in a nanosecond? Eliciting such a response was Alexander's special gift.

Alexander reached into his jacket pocket and drew out a simple paintbrush, one you might find in a child's watercolor set. He held it up. "Show me the moment you'd like to capture." He handed it to him.

The small wood brush was thin, almost disappearing between Eric's fingers. He ran a fingertip over the soft bristles at the end—not synthetic as he suspected, but of a fine sable. His nostrils filled with the oil paint of his old studio—a trick of his mind, of course. He hadn't picked up a brush in years, though oddly, the thought had occurred lately.

Alexander brought his arm to the back of the bench seat. His fingers, once inside Rebecca, now played with the back of her neck. "Show me."

Show him? It wasn't like Alexander to give vague instructions, so Eric would have to chance a move. If it wasn't what Alexander allowed and earned him a punishment, so be it. His agony at watching them touch each other, loving one another without him, couldn't be topped.

Eric placed his hand on Rebecca's knee and brought the paintbrush to her inner thigh.

"First," Eric said, "I'd start with her silhouette." The brush was light in his hand, but her leg quivered at the contact. It was intoxicating, this ability to make another person shake and moan. He almost understood Alexander's need to be in control of it, though he himself didn't.

He dragged the brush through the wetness coating her inner thigh. "It's important to get the perspective right."

"I might move to her breasts next." He brought the brush up to her chest and circled each nipple once with the paintbrush end. Her back arched into the touch, and his cock, ever the dutiful partner, bobbed as if demanding a role.

He was gratified to see Alexander's erection showed no signs of abating, either.

"I'd want to spend a great deal of time here." He brought the brush to her pussy, swirling the end along her crease.

Ran it up and down a few times until Rebecca was huffing out long moans.

He kept an eye on Alexander's movements, his reactions from under his lashes. The need for his approval always ran under the surface of his skin, twenty-four-seven. But at times like that, he burned for the man's acceptance. If granted, Eric would know he wasn't dreaming. He really was there.

Rebecca's breath hitched anew, the leather squeaking as she clutched at the bench. Her scent, rich and heady, in the small, enclosed space made his head spin a little.

Then, the colors began to form in his mind—mostly golds and greens, colors he'd always associated with Rebecca. The first time he'd laid eyes on her, he thought, "Elven princess." It'd been a long while since he'd allowed his imagination to run free. When did he stop painting? Years ago? Longer? Time didn't operate the same in Alexander's world.

He continued to lazily draw imaginary lines of color, now mixing in blues and yellow in his mind's eye—along Rebecca's thighs, belly, and labia. A dream-like quality settled over him—as if he wasn't there, yet he was.

Alexander shifted on the seat bench, breaking into his fog. He'd grabbed a fistful of her hair. "Make her come like this, Eric. And, Rebecca, don't hold back."

Permission granted, he yanked her leg open farther, so her labia was fully opened to him. He swirled and circled the brush right where she wanted. A bright yellow and orange sun bursting out of his mind's eyes mixed with the glistening pink. She was truly a sunset now, perched next to Alexander—as still and gold as the moon emerges in the twilight.

She released almost immediately—a reckless, beautiful release that had her clutching at Alexander's arm with one hand and the back of the limo bench with the other as her hips bucked upward.

The colors that danced in his consciousness soon shifted from the bright reds and oranges to something quieter, like the steel gray of a lake with a light blue in the sky overhead. He blinked hard and brought the brush down to settle against his knee. He was still rock hard, but something inside him had loosened.

Alexander's icy blue eyes filled his vision. "Well done."

He blinked up at the man. His vocal cords had long ago stopped working.

Alexander took the paintbrush from his fingers and flicked it to the floor. "I'd like you to get started tomorrow. I will watch you work"—he ran a fingertip down the side of Rebecca's breast—"as Rebecca poses."

He then grasped Eric's hand and molded his fingers around Alexander's erection. "And once it's done, we will have a celebration. All three of us."

Chapter Three

REBECCA

Rebecca's body strung tight. Every muscle, sinew, and tendon was strained, fighting its position. That was what happened when you sat for a portrait and didn't move for thirty minutes.

"Wider."

If Rebecca widened her knees any farther, she would be in a full split. She endeavored to obey Alexander's order anyway. In moments like that, her body would follow Alexander's lead as if tied to him by puppet strings.

Her arms shook as she leaned against them, her legs spread wide, revealing even more of herself.

She studied Alexander's eyes. As soon as she'd been positioned like that, he'd asked for them in his indomitable way. *"Give me your eyes."* His silky voice matched his presence so perfectly it was almost as if he weren't real.

But he was real.

Many people revered Alexander over the years. But they would never know him as well as she. She'd seen the nearly-invincible man vulnerable—when he was younger and hadn't yet shaped himself to be the indomitable Alexander Rockingham.

But even then, vulnerable or not, she'd never seen him weak. Not even forty years ago, standing outside the Wynter's locked gate trying to get inside to her and their shared dying lover, Charles. Today, she doubted he would ever let something as feeble as a sixteen-foot iron gate stand between her and Eric.

She ached to swat the old memories away, staying present.

It was futile.

She drank in the icy blue sky that seemed to float perpetually in Alexander's eyes. They were the most alive eyes she'd ever seen.

To think she and Alexander had been separated for decades until a few years ago. How had she survived that time? How had she breathed?

Perhaps that was why she'd always been so tired back then. Her energy had had a singular purpose during those lonely years: Don't think about Alexander. Now, that was all she did. Thought about him—and Eric, who only had his legs visible behind the wide canvas on which he painted.

Any women's magazine would tell you never to make men the center of your life. But those editors had never met those two men.

"Steady," Alexander's voice rumbled.

Her knees had begun to quiver. They would. The love of her life stood before her, had taken her to the precipice of coming many times over the last forty-eight hours—but not allowed her to release. *Steady* wasn't possible.

First, he'd denied her an orgasm last night. Then in his office. Then after one orgasm, he brought her up to the precipice again in the limousine. They circled the Capitol Building *sixteen times* (yes, she'd counted) before they were back where they started—at Club Accendos. Though, that time, in their private rooms upstairs. Instead of finishing her, Alexander delayed again. He wanted Eric to paint her portrait first.

Alexander glanced down at the canvas that blocked most of Eric from her sight. Only his legs showed—bare legs. Of course, he hadn't allowed the man to wear a stitch of clothing as he painted her portrait. She imagined his cock standing at full attention behind that canvas. The thought only made her thighs wetter.

Alexander murmured. "Beautiful choice of color." She didn't know if he referred to what he saw in the picture or Eric.

Great. Now, she could only think of Eric's incredible body. Men. They only got hotter with age.

The silver had deepened at Alexander's temples and around that magnificent organ, unavailable to her right now. But the lines around his forehead and eyes had softened since the day she'd reconnected with him.

Focus, she reminded herself. Stop thinking about the past.

Eric made an unhappy sound, a kind of deep grunt as if displeased about something. Her belly jumped a little. Perhaps he wasn't inspired by her like that—splayed out, available.

"Everything okay?" She couldn't help but ask the question.

Neither man answered. Instead, Alexander placed his large hand on Eric's shoulder, and the man's legs quivered. She didn't need to see him to see how his whole body might be trembling.

Alexander moved to stand behind him. He was so tall that his head rose above the canvas perched on the easel, but the bulk of him vanished behind the picture. A long moan came out of Eric, and his legs shot out straight as if jolted with electricity. What were they doing back there?

"Rebecca, stay where you are." Alexander knew her so well, knew her urge to jump off the small chaise to do just that.

A small grumble came out of Eric, followed by soft thumps. It was the sound of flesh being batted about. Her imagination fired. Alexander was teasing him. Maybe torturing him.

Alexander's head reappeared as he straightened. His blue eyes met hers as his gaze honed on her anew. "Much better. Eric now matches you in that gorgeous color."

Alexander emerged from behind the canvas and was at her feet in two strides. He smiled down at her. "Now, how about a little inspiration for Eric? To keep him standing tall? Touch yourself."

He spun on his heel and seated himself in a chair next

to where Eric worked.

She brought her dominant hand between her legs.

"No, your other hand."

Oh great. It would take her twice as long if she had to use her left. Then again, she had been in this position for so long that her fingers were practically numb. Anyone who'd ever sat for a painting knew fifteen minutes could seem like fifteen hours. But she did what he asked, so grateful that he would allow herself to finally come.

She quickened her fingers, eager for a release.

Alexander leaned farther back into his chair. "Tell me when you're close."

Damn it. She'd be told to stop again, wouldn't she?

Within minutes, her body was on that edge, that glorious spot where you knew you were about to come. And whether strong or weak, a beautiful release of tension would follow.

But she was a good girl. At least, she tried to be.

Ha, girl. At her age?

"Close," she eked out.

"Still your fingers, Rebecca."

A shot of anger lit up her body from toes to hair. Alexander's cruel streak was on fire today. But she had asked for his dominance when perched on his office desk. She had practically begged him for it.

Then he did something she didn't expect. He rose. Removed his jacket. Draped it over the chair. Rolled up his shirt sleeves. He took his sweet time doing it, of course, revealing his flesh to her inch by inch. As he bared his forearms, the soft sound of fabric joined the *swiff-swiff-swiff* of Eric's brush moving over the canvas.

The man may be in his early sixties, but he was beyond beautiful. He took good care of himself, and it showed. Hard muscle that glided under skin and hair peppered with silver.

Two strides, and again, he was before her. He hooked a hand under each of her knees and twisted her so she back fell against the chaise's curved side.

Alexander unbuckled his pants. "Eric, do you have enough to finish without seeing Rebecca?"

She craned her neck around Alexander and caught a glimpse of Eric appearing from behind the canvas. Nude. Beautifully erect. Flushed from head to toe. A wash of red paint smeared on one thigh. "I do. I can finish here without Rebecca sitting for it. I have her memorized."

"Very good." Alexander never stopped staring at her. "Come join us. And Rebecca, love. Open your mouth."

He didn't have to ask twice.

"You did so well during our little car ride. I'd like you to do the same for Eric."

She loved being with Eric as much as she loved being with Alexander, but that was not what she had in mind. Eric either. A flicker of disappointment rose in his eyes. Eric loved her. She was certain of it. But Alexander so infrequently gave himself to the man, his eyes drooping a bit at being given over to her instead of him was justified.

Eric, however, didn't hesitate to appear by her head. She lifted her chin and let her head fall back. He fed himself to her open mouth.

He was not as thick and long as Alexander, but her heart sang with every inch he offered.

She sucked him in a little deeper as Alexander straddled

the chaise and entered her in one long smooth stroke. He was always so careful, knowing her body required more care now. Her desires, however, had not abated one bit.

Alexander moved in. Eric moved out. Alexander back in. And together, they started a rhythm.

Her hands moved up to Eric's thighs, not to push him away but to draw him closer. He also was too hesitant with her, as if she were made of spun sugar. Serving these two men at once was a rare gift, one she wished they'd take—with more force.

But her prayers were soon answered. The thrusts grew longer, deeper. The climb back up to the ecstasy ladder was easy. Her mouth was too full to ask permission to come. She would just have to risk it because there was no way in hell she would be able to hold anything back, not when they glided in and out of her with such conviction. *Finally.*

"Eric," Alexander growled. "Eyes on me."

The thought of the two men gazing at each other was ultimately what did it. She came—hard. Sounds reverberated in her throat, and her legs twitched.

Alexander's chuckle soon filled the air, followed by a quick grunt of his own. He filled her completely, as did Eric, and they both finished inside her together.

As Eric drew himself out, she caught her breath, her cheeks wet with her own saliva and tears. A thought sliced through her brain. A vision so clear she nearly forgot to keep breathing. It was the answer to a question that had been roiling in her brain—what was next for the three of them?

They'd had a glorious eleven months on the road, being together, loving one another, like three puzzle pieces that formed a whole. But something had roughened the edges of those pieces lately. Perhaps it was their re-entry into reality? Or was it something deeper?

But now, she suddenly, inexplicably, knew what to do to smooth those rough spots again.

She blinked up at Alexander, who cocked his head. "Rebecca?"

"Thank you, Sir."

His smile returned. "What else is going on inside that beautiful head of yours?"

"Nothing." And everything.

She couldn't wait to see the portrait Eric painted of her. It would be a constant reminder of the moment when an idea fell into her mind—one that would finally fulfill their destinies, one that would seal them together forever.

Chapter Four

ERIC

Eric shook his head. "I can't." He stamped his feet as if that would keep the circulation going in his limbs. If he'd known Rebecca would want them to huddle in the far corner of Accendos' walled garden, he'd have put on a thicker jacket. Given the icy wind, his gonads might be frozen forever.

"And why not?" Rebecca widened her stance and crossed her arms over her breasts—still glorious, even if hidden by a fleece. "A portrait of Alexander when administering a scene would go for—"

"Hundreds of thousands. I know that." But paint his portrait? While dominating someone?

How did he explain it to her? For the last year, as they'd traveled, he'd itched to capture Alexander's essence on a canvas, not just wielding his dominance like a Samurai sword but, well, doing anything.

But oil paint on a canvas could never contain the man. How did one catch the exact blue of his eyes, especially when they deepened like a sea about to break over a levy when a correction was required? Or the way the light ignited the silver in his hair as he circled a willing submissive, deciding what he'd like to do next? Eric's mind went to mush just thinking about doing the man justice.

The frost had left intricate patterns on the grass tufts under his feet. That was when he realized his gaze had dropped. Such an automatic reaction even when thinking about Alexander.

Rebecca's hand cupped his chin and raised his face. Her eyes held too much concern. "What's wrong, really?" she asked.

The genuine problem with painting Alexander was deeper, wasn't it? Eric slipped too easily into Alexander's thrall when he was in full Master mode. How the hell would he be able to hold a drafting pencil when his fingers ached to reach for his cock—or Alexander's. Or any part of Rebecca. Anything to connect with them both.

He took her fingers, surprisingly warm in the cold, in his. "I love the idea of the three of us starting a mentoring program at Accendos." That had been the bait on her fishing line to lure him in. The idea of starting a school for people like them. "I'd trust no one more than Alexander to teach the next generation of people like us. Hell, even having an art auction to raise money for it. But what you're asking me to do …"

He spun away. He couldn't do it. His feet crunched the brittle limestone pebbles under his feet as he headed back to the house.

Rebecca jogged alongside him, her breath leaving a hazy entrail in the frigid air. "You think his ego doesn't need it. But people around him need it."

"People?"

Her hand gripped his arm frantically. "Please."

"That's not what I'm thinking at all. I have no painting skills when he's in full … Alexander mode."

"Who does?" She chewed her bottom lip. If anyone understood, it would be her. "But you could try." She dropped her hand and gestured for him to follow her. "Do you have a notebook on you right now?"

She knew he did.

His hand found its way to his backside, and he felt for the small black moleskin he kept in the back pocket of his jeans. It was a comfort to find the flat surface there. Inspiration could strike at any time. The old spark had somehow been ignited recently. Ever since he'd painted Rebecca a few weeks ago, his hands needed to sketch and capture everyone around him. Everyone except Alexander.

The sound of a branch snapping off a distant tree sounded—probably from being weighed down by ice. He understood the feeling.

She took a big breath, letting it out in a white cloud that hovered before her face. "Your lips are turning blue. Let's go inside." She slipped her arm into his and led him back toward the house.

She still walked too slowly. "Do you know the hardest

part about being separated from Alexander for all those years? It was not knowing if he was happy. If he was living the way he wanted to. Even apart, he was ubiquitous in my life. There wasn't a day I didn't think of him. Like he was gently guiding me all the time just by existing."

Eric understood that. Even when not physically in the room, Alexander was present.

"And it's the same for so many people." She drew closer to him. "He doesn't realize what he's done for the people who cross the threshold of this place. So about my school idea … If he could mentor the next generation, well …"

"He'd find a larger purpose." While the man had plenty of it to go around, they knew Alexander. If he wasn't expanding, he didn't feel he was doing enough.

"And"—she cocked her head. Oh no. He recognized the storm brewing in her gray eyes— "you and I can offer ourselves to be the demo leaders, which means …"

One side of Eric's lips inched up. Finally, blessed warmth spread through his body like wildfire at the thought of Alexander using them as his stand-ins. "That's the best part of the idea." Being handled by Alexander in any way, shape, or form was too good of an opportunity to pass up. Still didn't mean he'd be able to paint the man doing it. "We can still raise funds without a painting."

"Not as quickly or as much. Just consider what I said. We'd get there so much faster." Her warm hand slipped into his. She raised it up to her mouth, and she sent hot breath over his skin as if to warm him.

"I will."

A sly smirk formed on her face. He was an idiot to say

yes, but stopping Rebecca from egging him on? Futile. The woman was as stubborn as Alexander. Scratch that. Maybe worse.

They strode toward the Library, where they knew they'd find Alexander. As soon as they stepped into the large archway, Eric's gaze alighted on the back of Alexander's head, the silver in his black hair shining under dimmed lighting. He sat in an armchair witnessing the scenes playing out in the room. The club had relaxed since Alexander had been traveling with him and Rebecca. However, *relaxed* wasn't how Alexander had wanted his home-turned-club to operate.

A woman in the far corner keened as a ginger-haired man, someone Eric didn't recognize, twisted her nipple with some force. The day had started early. Saturdays were like that at Club Accendos.

A man, blindfolded, kneeled five feet before Alexander. Another young man with a toss of dark hair over his forehead was bent at the waist. Whatever the guy said, it elicited quite a reaction from the lucky bastard showing himself off to Alexander. The blindfolded one shuddered from head to foot.

Rebecca dropped his hand, marched up to Alexander, and hard-dropped to the pillow beside his chair. She bent her head. Alexander didn't flinch at the intrusion. Mild but still an interruption.

"Can we talk?" she mouthed. Still no response. His eyes remained firmly aimed at the scene unfolding. It was only when the woman in the corner loudly moaned did he raise his chin. Blinked twice.

Rebecca inched closer and laid her head on his knee. Her hand reached for his shoe, an expensive pair of Italian leather loafers. Eric swallowed hard when Rebecca snaked her hand up under his trouser leg. What was she doing?

Eric only had to move six inches to the left to see Alexander's face in a mirror reflection—a large, ungodly thing with a thick gold frame.

Rebecca opened her mouth to speak, and Alexander raised his index finger. "Stop," he said to Rebecca. At least, that was what Eric thought he said. He'd read the man's lips.

In true Rebecca fashion, she didn't stop, however. She pushed off the floor, rose, and circled behind the chair. She placed her hands on Alexander's shoulders, leaned down, and ran her hands down his chest. One hand slipped inside his shirt. She then mouthed something in his ear that Eric couldn't hear or lip-read.

His icy blue eyes remained fixed on the couple before him.

Eric had spent countless hours studying Alexander's cues. The set of his jaw, the way his right pinky finger and ring finger rubbed together to move the ring on his hand. There was one subtle gesture Eric would avoid at all costs—a small muscle in his left cheek that throbbed when displeased. Alexander's chest expanded in a long inhale. And that muscle? A slight twitch formed.

When Alexander raised another finger, the dark-haired man nodded once at him. Alexander then divested himself of Rebecca's hands and rose from the chair. "Rebecca, here."

Alexander stripped people bare with his penetrating gaze, no matter the scenario. It gave nothing away yet said everything at once. It was as if he knew things—things about you. But now? His eyes fired like blue lightning. Skin-searing. Bone-boiling. It'd stop the earth from rotating.

Rebecca had overplayed her hand, interrupting him. And why the devil was it so important to have broached the subject of starting a mentorship program immediately? The man was busy. He wanted the man's attention, but it was too much.

Eric could spin on his heel and head upstairs. Let her deal with the consequences. Or should he stay? He never failed to worry about her. She was so reckless sometimes. Impatient. Demanding.

Other times, she came across like a little bird, delicate, as if she might snap if handled too harshly. He'd yet to see what constituted "too harsh," however. She'd often told him and Alexander they did nothing with her she didn't crave.

He slunk along the inside of the library. When he could finally see Alexander's face, the man's eyes sliced to him for a moment, then back to Rebecca, who circled to face him. She smiled up at him. Devious. Not at all sorry.

He gazed down at her. "Someone interested in play?"

"Yes, please."

His large hand descended on her cheek. His fingers then raked backward to grab a fistful of her hair. He yanked her head back, and her lips dropped open. He half dragged, half led her around to the back of the chair. Then he unceremoniously pushed her forward so her body had no choice but to drape over the back of the chair.

"So watch." He kicked her legs wider, making her splay her palms on the seat cushion to keep from face-planting.

He then positioned himself between her legs but didn't touch a single part of her. "Eyes on the scene, Rebecca. Maybe you'll learn something."

Rebecca's eyes glanced upward at Eric. He'd slunk so far around the library that he was startled when his back hit the old library ladder that rested against the tall bookshelves. He leaned against the sturdy wood thing.

He didn't know where to look. The scenes unfolding around him? Because any order Alexander gave Rebecca, he often obeyed in solidarity. It had become a natural state—the partnership between him and Rebecca with one sole goal—love Alexander, abide by Alexander.

Or perhaps he should watch the man himself? Eric flushed from head to toe at witnessing Alexander in his element, like a schoolboy. It was all that talk about painting his portrait and the reasons he'd always fail at it.

Rebecca's gray eyes caught his once more, and she mouthed one word. "Draw."

Ah, the devil's mistress had nothing on her. She was trying to inspire him, perhaps?

Still, why not? It would be futile, but at least it'd give his hands something to do other than drift places it should not, like his hardening cock.

He reached into his back pocket and drew out the small notebook. Then into his jacket pocket. He found an ink pen. Not at all what he should use, but no one had to see the scribbles.

"Are you watching, Rebecca?" Alexander's words cut into the air. He wasn't looking at her. Rather his gaze wandered around the room as if taking in all the scenes.

Like the strongest oak standing in a forest of saplings.

When she didn't answer his question, his large hand reached out and slapped her on the ass. The smack, muffled a bit by her pants, reverberated around the room.

She inhaled sharply. "Yes, Sir. What would you like me to see?"

His brow furrowed. Displeased with her question? The lines softened across his forehead. "See what I see. Power. Pain. Pleasure. *Discipline*."

Alexander didn't see people the same way mere mortals did, like their hair color or height. He tuned into their energy. Call it aura-reading. Call it mind-reading. It didn't matter. Eventually, he ferreted out what they wanted and needed.

Rebecca's lips parted. "I see you in everything here." Her eyes drifted closed as if she was a sated kitten in a slice of sunshine.

As if they were linked, Eric's lids grew heavy, his eyes closing. Sounds floated all around him. The soft whisper of air moving in and out of his lungs. Soft moans to the right. The slap of flesh ringing. Small murmurs.

Fabric drew closer. His eyes snapped open. It'd been a trick of his mind—or ears. Alexander stared at him. His spine straightened another inch, and his nostrils flared. He wasn't angry, however. He was just being himself. Noticing everything. Taking in *everything and everyone*.

Eric's hand hovered over the notebook. He'd been scratching something. He didn't bother to glance down. Doodles, nothing more.

His gaze softened. His pen scratches soon mixed with the moans, the rustle of fabric, and the heavy breathing all around. He didn't even know what he was drawing at that point. Something far more important caught his attention— an Alexander he hadn't considered before. A level of dominance he was shocked he hadn't tuned into.

Alexander drank in all the scenes like a lion might assess its pride. He was in control of every scene in the room. His presence allowed them to continue, explore, and take it as far as they had consented to—all because he'd not have it any other way. His gaze kept them on watch. And he could stop them at any time.

Rebecca was right. Alexander was everywhere. A merciless energy field that cradled you and sometimes pushed you. But always loved you.

He looked down at his paper and was stunned to see what he'd drawn. A face with eyes so piercing, Eric nearly stepped backward.

Alexander's voice rang out. "Rebecca, Eric."

His gaze lifted to the man. "Do you two want to tell me what you're in cahoots about?"

Eric pushed off the ladder and let his legs carry him forward until he stood by the two of them. An odd calm had settled in his belly. "Rebecca has an idea." And for reasons he would never understand, he lifted the notebook and showed it to Alexander.

He waited in a submissive silence for him to study it. Eric's heart thudded heavily in his chest. "It's not right. It's just a draft." He could never stay silent for long.

The man's lips inched up. "It's good." His gaze returned to assessing the room. "I was waiting for you to do that. And to learn more about this mentorship program that you two have been whispering about."

Alexander knew what they were planning? Or had Rebecca already told him, and it was a set-up?

Eric and Rebecca locked eyes for a second. She smiled at him.

Alexander filled his chest with air. "I like it. Now, sit." His gaze dipped to the pillow Rebecca had abandoned. "Sketch more."

At that moment, he didn't care how the man found out. Alexander had just asked him to draw. A glow started deep in his pelvis and traveled up his spine before making its way down his arms. Alexander wanted to be sketched, and as if jolted by life-giving electricity, his fingers twitched around the pen he'd clutched.

Maybe he'd finally been given what he didn't know he needed: Permission.

Eric settled himself on the pillow. Opened to a new page.

Alexander granted him another look. "When you're done, ask me what inspiration you need to finish, and we will do whatever it takes."

He sent a silent prayer to the gods and goddesses of artists and released it like smoke to the heavens. Let his sketch not be good enough. Let it require all the inspiration Alexander could dole out.

Rebecca has said "people" needed the portrait. She'd meant him, hadn't she?

Chapter Five

ERIC

He waited two days before addressing it. "It" being Alexander's statement.

"When you're done, ask me what inspiration you need to finish, and we will do whatever it takes."

He tried a dozen times to make himself go to Alexander's office, make an appointment to show him how much he'd be willing to let the man be in control. He could always say "no," then. But he couldn't make himself do it.

Instead, he was striding down the long hallway alongside the set of French doors that led out to the garden on his way to a yoga class in the gym when he rounded the corner and ran smack into the man himself.

Alexander chuckled and grabbed him by both arms. "Coming or going to meet Rebecca?" He knew Eric so well.

Eric spent most of his time with the woman, if not with Alexander. It was as if a piece of him was missing if he wasn't in the same room with at least one of them.

"Want to go to the dungeon with me?" The question just blurted out.

Alexander blinked once. He'd taken him by surprise. A sliver of satisfaction that Eric had caught him off guard touched a part of him. Another part inside curled into a ball over the fact the question wasn't met with immediate enthusiasm.

Alexander murmured. "Tempting."

"Please." He might as well go straight into begging. Eric ran a hand through his hair. "I mean, it's been a while. And whatever you want, of course."

"I was on my way to the Library. We've got some new people in, and Master R asked—"

"I can help." He swallowed down any more words. Alexander's lids lowered a fraction. To most, the move was imperceptible. To Eric? A note of displeasure from the man, and it sent shivers up his spine. "I mean …"

"Yes." Alexander's chin raised slightly. "I do believe you can help. Follow." The man strode past him. Eric had to quicken his steps considerably to keep up with Alexander's long strides. At six foot five, he could be down the hallway in seconds.

As soon as they entered the large room, Alexander swung his gaze at Eric. "Any new limits?"

The man had to ask? But, dear God, let his question mean what he thought it did. "None."

Alexander nodded once and stepped inside.

The Library wasn't busy. Even if it were, picking out the newcomers, a couple, was easy. A tall brunette in a white cream suit and blue corset peeking out between her lapels picked at her cuticles. Her companion, shorter than her by a good six inches, had his arms crossed. Eric caught him nervously drumming his fingers against his ribcage. Who could blame them?

Club Accendos was one of the few environments in Washington where inhibitions and judgment had no place. Sexual freedom was a given. It could be disconcerting to be surrounded by people exercising that liberty with gusto.

Alexander strode over to the couple. Eric followed.

The woman flushed from head to toe and cast her eyes down as Alexander neared. Her companion gazed directly at Alexander. The dynamic was clear as to who was Dominant in the relationship.

"Claude. Jeanette." Alexander nodded once. "Welcome."

The man visibly relaxed and held out his hand. "Thank you for the invitation. You've got quite the place here."

"This is Eric." Alexander gestured to him.

Eric held out his hand, which Claude took. "I've heard there's a third, as well?"

The man's interest in their personal dynamic irritated him. It wasn't unusual for Club members to ask where Rebecca was if not with Alexander or Eric. Something about Claude's tone, however … He suddenly felt like a consolation prize.

"Rebecca. She's busy," Eric didn't know if she was busy or not, but hell if he'd stand there in second place.

Alexander didn't react to his words. "I understand you have a particular interest in rope work."

"We've ... dabbled."

Jeanette flushed an even deeper crimson.

Alexander eyed her, then sliced his gaze back to Claude. "Care to witness how I would approach it?"

The man's face fell in shock. He swallowed hard and nodded once. Ah, so he got the incredible honor Alexander was about to bestow on him. He hadn't played in the Library, and certainly not with witnesses, in years—long before Eric was graced with the man's heart. Or so he'd been told.

Alexander drew in a long breath, and his eyes fired. An untrained eye, one not used to assessing every molecule of Alexander's being like Eric was, wouldn't have caught the shift in him. Eric, however, hummed with electricity, fully aware he, too, was about to get a supreme gift. He would witness whatever Alexander planned. At least, that was what he was sure his presence was for.

But then, as Alexander did so often, he surprised him. The man turned to him. "Eric. Choose your ropes."

Choose. And *your*. Alexander wanted him to bottom for him? Eric hurried to the large credenza on the far wall. It held many things. Eric found skeins of silk, hemp, or jute ropes. Which one would Alexander want? Silk was softer, looser. Jute was uncomfortable as shit. Then there were five- and six-millimeter diameter choices. A subtle difference that would determine so much; namely, the length of play, given the thickness would dictate how long his limbs would hold out.

"Eric?" Alexander asked calmly.

He was taking too long. He grabbed two skeins of hemp with six-millimeter thickness in black. No way would he have chosen the hot pink, which was the only other choice in that combination.

He handed the bundles to Alexander. "Do you consent to rope bondage—"

"I consent to non-consent." That left the playing field wide open.

Alexander's lips quirked. "Eager."

The man had no idea. Eric merely swallowed and nodded once.

Alexander turned to Claude. "Do you know what that means?"

"I do."

"Then have a seat. Over there." Alexander gestured to the largest leather chair in the room. The man would be dwarfed by it. Perhaps a message? There was one lion in the room, and it wasn't Claude. Still, the man settled into the chair. Jeanette knelt next to it.

Alexander moved to a series of hooks that hung from the ceiling a mere twenty-five feet from where the couple sat. Eric followed.

Alexander turned to him, a skein in each hand. "Are you sure about this?"

"Never surer."

"Then say it. Loud enough for it to reach everyone's ears."

Eric widened his stance. "I consent to non-consent to Master Alexander Rockingham." He nearly bellowed the words. If anyone missed it, they were either in subspace or deaf.

Alexander never took his eyes off his face. "Carrie?"

"I witness, Master Rockingham. CNC. Noted." Carrie's strong voice reached his ears, but he nearly didn't believe it. When had Carrie entered? Then again, the submissive assistant was a fixture at Accendos and had learned to be stealthier than a panther.

Eric's gaze began to drift downward. So, his submission began. He was a switch and could move from role to role if given enough incentive. With Alexander, his mere presence was enough. But when in his full Master power? He had no choice. It just happened.

"Claude," Alexander continued. "A witness to consent is a requirement."

"I've been told," the man said.

"Good. One violation and membership is revoked forever."

Eric dearly would have loved to see the man's reaction to that statement, but he couldn't rip his eyes off Alexander's chest, his hands holding the ropes. Soon, those ropes would be on him, and who knew what would happen then? He began to harden. It would be damned difficult to remember it was a demonstration. Merely a demo, he repeated in his head.

"CNC. Hmmm." Alexander's hand lifted his chin.

Eric had surprised him. "Yes, Sir." Alexander knew him—his limits, his desires, when anything became too much. He'd only give one person on the planet such control over him, and he stood before him.

One small nod from Alexander acknowledged his offer.

"Remember. You are mine." His eyes softened.

An abnormal level of joy filled Eric's chest. Alexander agreed with his statement, yes. But more than that, the man's tone was different. Alexander often declared his ownership of him and Rebecca. But right then, his voice had relaxed, was even tender. It didn't last. Alexander's eyes shuttered back to that fire-ice blue.

Alexander's hand dropped. "Clothes off. And watch me as you shed them." He dropped to a chair that Carrie had dragged over. A simple wooden schoolhouse chair that creaked under the man's considerable size. He set the skeins on his lap and adjusted his suit coat, a quick jerk of his sleeves that went straight to Eric's crotch and growing erection.

Eric yanked his belt free and raised one eyebrow as if to question where he should drop it. He half hoped the man would ask for it to use on him later. Anything to be handled by him.

Alexander nodded and sliced his eyes to the floor, a quick up and back in answer. Eric obeyed. First, the belt clattered to the floor. Then his jacket. His shirt was next, followed quickly by pants and briefs. He kicked them to the side with some force, which elicited a tiny smile from Alexander. A true submissive would have been more timid.

Alexander cocked his head to look around him. "Claude. Eric has a pain level of eight, and I do believe he's testing me to see if I might try to wipe away that sliver of bravado. What do you think?"

Shit, no. Asking for the man's input? He didn't give a rat's ass what Claude thought. Shame began to build inside him.

"I don't know. I don't know Eric." It was the best answer—correct, humble, and wise, given Alexander was also testing Claude's arrogance. Eric tried to tamp down the irritation that had bubbled up a second ago because Alexander was right. Eric was trying to show off a little. But he didn't want Alexander to hold back just because there were witnesses.

Alexander upturned his palm. Carrie, who Eric had barely registered, handed him something silver, metal. Fuck him. A cock cage?

The infernal thing was on him in seconds, leather straps keeping it snug and tight. Alexander then tightened it even more. His cock pulsed against the long steel pillars.

"Thank you, Sir," he said.

"Knees."

Eric fell to the oriental carpet before Alexander and bowed his head, trying desperately to ignore his growing hard-on now bobbing from the drop, the skin biting into the metal. He studied the man's Dior derby shoes, a dark brown and shined to perfection, and waited.

For long minutes, nothing was said. Just the scratch of a five-o'clock shadow across a chin. Alexander's. Eric conjured up the image of the man rubbing his finger along it, assessing him. That only got him harder, the devil cage fighting it.

Finally, Alexander rose. The rustle of fabric was next. "Eric, look at me."

Alexander shed his jacket. "I want you to look at me the whole time. Your whole world shows in your eyes."

What the hell did that mean? He didn't bother to puzzle it out because Alexander began to roll up his sleeves. He revealed his strong forearms dusted with silver inch by inch. It was the hottest thing he'd seen in weeks.

Alexander picked up the ropes. "I should gag you."

"Whatever you want."

Alexander yanked one skein free and snapped it so the long rope spread out. "But I want your mouth available to me."

Cage or not, Eric's cock would explode right then and there in front of everyone. A small crowd had formed. In addition to Claude, Jeanette, and Carrie, others had filtered into the room. Word likely got out. He recognized the people, but his mind had shut out their names. It didn't matter.

"I see you like that idea." Alexander roughly grabbed his chin.

Right then, Eric was sure Alexander would rescind his idea. But he simply removed his hand and smiled down at him. With a snap of his wrist, another rope coil unfurled, the ends hitting the Oriental carpet in a soft *plunk*.

Alexander kept his eyes focused on his work. He looped two lengths of rope around Eric's rib cage, the restriction just on the right side of too much.

"You'll tell me if you get dizzy, right?" Alexander asked.

Eric nodded once, unable to rip his gaze from the concentration etched across the man's face. He had Alexander's full attention, which made his belly flutter like a schoolgirl's. Another yank and he gasped. Leaning now against Alexander's broad chest made his cock twitch with hunger—and pain.

More pulls around his sternum shifted his attention. Beautiful knots lay against his chest, the ends hanging loose like tentacles. Alexander's fingers slipped under the ropes, checking them. Such care nearly made Eric's eyes prick.

The slither of rope as Alexander continued to bind him, forcefully and mercilessly, awakened every nerve ending he had. He couldn't stop a moan from escaping his throat.

Alexander grasped his captured cock and held it. "I see you appreciate my work." As if Eric's swollen erection, now an angry red, could give any other message?

Another snap of rope across the carpet. For long minutes, Alexander worked on encasing his chest and arms. Pulls on the rope covering his torso had him swaying and pitching. Then one final harsh yank and both his arms were laced behind him. Could he free himself, if needed? He sucked in a long breath, the ropes stopping his chest from expanding. *No.* The cage bit into his cock as it began to pulse in frustration.

He'd been bound before—many times. But it'd been so long since he'd been handled by Alexander in that manner. He was in his full element, and Eric's body screamed for more.

If he had pined for the man before, the last year had turned him into an Alexander addict. When Alexander scened, he was all in. That was what had been missing for the last number of weeks: Alexander's full attention, Eric's drug of choice. And he was getting a fix right then. It only ratcheted up his craving.

Alexander rose to his full height and assessed his

work. "Beautiful, Eric. Spread those knees. Let us see your beautiful captive cock."

The words floated through his brain like water, but his knees widened, scratching against the carpet from his full weight, given his arms were no use in helping take any of the load.

Alexander slowly walked around him—once, twice. "Claude, see his skin all pink around the rope." At least, Eric thought that was what he said. He was growing spacey.

More words were bandied about between Alexander and Claude. Eric sucked in more air and tuned into the tight crunch of ropes around his chest and arms. Alexander had skills—and his assessment as he circled Eric made his mouth water.

As he shifted on his knees, the devil cock cage bit into him. Fuck, it hurt. And God, he wanted to be taken right then and there on the spot. Anywhere—mouth, ass. Just let him come.

Alexander chuckled, and his mouth just spit out some words.

The tips of Alexander's expensive shoes touched his knees. "What did you say?"

"Sadist." The word was true but bratty nonetheless. As if the man didn't know what he was? No one knew himself, grew fully *into* himself, more than Alexander.

Alexander's large hand engulfed his chin and lifted his face so high the skin under his neck stretched painfully. The rough ropes bit deliciously and scratched Eric's skin.

One side of the man's mouth lifted. "Care to stop?"

Eric's nostrils flared. Like hell. He sharply shook his

head as much as he could in Alexander's strong grip.

"Please, more." Eric didn't plead, but he was beyond having any pride. Bound, caged, at the mercy of the man. "And let me do something for you."

"You're doing it." Alexander pressed a kiss on his forehead, then let go of Eric's chin. His gaze fell to his captured cock. Precum leaked at the tip.

Alexander slipped fingers underneath a rope at his sternum. "Anything hurt?"

"No." Just his dick, which throbbed for attention.

Alexander assessed him. Said something to Claude. "Watch the skin color, always."

"Not enough," Eric gritted out, raising his gaze to his tormentor and the object of his full lust.

Alexander peered down at him. "Oh? Perhaps I'll leave you here. Let Carrie watch you as you reassess."

"I'm sorry, Master. Please. I'm sorry."

Alexander leaned over him, roughly pitching his hips against him. The man was hard as a rock. Alexander was turned on. Maybe he wanted him, too? But didn't think he could?

"You can have me," Eric bit out. It wasn't exactly what he meant to say, but it was all he could manage.

Alexander pitched his hips against him again. "This isn't yours today."

Pent-up anger filled every inch of Eric's insides. Alexander wanted him, yet he'd deny him? Normally, his feelings didn't ride under his skin that much. But the man had unleashed a longing in him, like a child yearning for attention after being ignored for too long.

He wanted to cry out, scream, let out all the *more-more-more* that was filling his head. Instead, he bit down on his bottom lip so hard blood, tasting like salt and rust, coated his tongue.

Alexander leaned down, the fabric of his shirt fabric touching Eric's back. "You want me to fuck you, don't you?"

Was he kidding? Of course, he did. "Please. Yes."

He tried to turn around to face the man, but he was held fast. Alexander pushed Eric's face down. Rough carpet scratched his cheek as Alexander's large hand held his neck, the other lifting Eric's hips.

"Ass up, brat," Alexander growled. "You declared CNC? Then you take what I offer."

The ropes made it impossible for Eric to fight against the position. But he tried. Writhed and tried to roll like a cat. Alexander anticipated every move, his hands now on both sides of Eric's hips. He couldn't have pushed up if he'd tried.

Something cold filled his ass. Lube. Something fell to the carpet next to him, but it wasn't in view.

"Take what I choose to give you." Alexander parted his buttocks and pushed in a butt plug. Raw fire possessed him as Alexander ground it home. "All of it."

Fuck, it hurt. They'd done it before, but not that rough and with something so large, and it'd been so long. But God help him, a longing to be reamed raw arose. Eric grunted and growled at the invasion, at the pain that mixed with the need for more. He pushed back, a signal he was all in on the new development. A sharp crack on his ass was his answer.

Alexander was in charge. Hell, when wasn't he? And Eric had declared CNC.

A sob formed in his throat—emotion from the last month that had been stuffed down. He snarled, his breath wet as saliva ran down his cheek to his chin before falling to the carpet. Alexander pulled the thick butt plug out and pitched it back in again and again.

Then, Alexander's hand wound into Eric's hair, pulling his head up from the carpet. "Tell me how much you want it."

As if his cock painfully swollen in its prison wasn't enough? "Master. Alexander." He ground his ass backward.

An infernal chuckle came out of Alexander. It burned Eric.

More words left his mouth. "Don't want the job yourself?" Eric was being a huge brat. He didn't care. The man could have fucked him senseless, but he was choosing not to.

Alexander's voice softened. "Unnecessary."

Eric knew what he meant. He was being greedy, trying to force more from the man. It was ungrateful—and futile. He'd wanted a scene with him for the last month. He got it. It should be enough.

Alexander pulled out the plug and let it clatter to the floor. Then he yanked on the ropes until stinging blood rushed to where Eric's limbs had been restricted. Strong arms held Eric up as the ropes fell away one wrap at a time.

God, he was lightheaded. Someone held up a water bottle to him. Large hands. It was Alexander. He was leaning against his chest, so cold. Something warm engulfed him next. A blanket?

He didn't know how long they sat there in the middle of the Library. The crowd had dispersed, and Carrie stepped forward. Alexander waved her off but took the offered robe. "I've got it." Alexander helped him up, then slipped Eric's arms into each sleeve. He swayed, but Alexander kept him close.

He remembered walking down hallways and then entering their bedroom. He was led to the bed and crawled under sheets held open for him.

Alexander's concerned face stared down at him.

He grasped Alexander's arm. "I'm sorry."

"You never have to say that to me. You did well."

A puff of air left his nostrils. "You never have to say that to me." He was tired. Or maybe he was giving up.

Alexander's hand fell to his cheek. "You honored me today."

"Oh, yeah?" His words were lazy, as if his tongue wasn't working properly.

"You offered me full control." He rose. "Sleep. You need it. And Eric …"

That made his eyes snap open, even though he desperately wanted to sleep.

"For the record, and I'm only saying this to you. And only once. I don't want to work this much anymore, either. But it's …"

"Necessary?"

"Yes, and you're helping me more than you know."

Renewed shame filled him. "Thank you. I'm—"

"Important to me."

Erik had wanted to say, *I'm honored. I know what you had to do. He'd been a brat. Alexander, you did what you were supposed to do. Showed them how it works.* But he couldn't help wishing it'd gone another way. Then again, wishing was for fools. In the end, no words came to him. So, he merely let his eyes drift closed. Somehow, he slept.

Later that night, in the dark, a deep dip in the mattress caused him to startle awake. Alexander was finally coming to bed. He crawled between him and Rebecca, who stretched like a kitten and rolled toward him as if her body was also attuned to Alexander's presence. Alexander drew Eric closer, his large form engulfing him. Rebecca's legs touched his as she swung her leg over the two of them. It was her signal. She wanted them.

Alexander grasped Eric's hand and pulled it to his cock, hard as a rock. Arousal hit him hard. He rolled to his side, facing Alexander. The man's eyes glittered in the dark, capturing the garden's night lights slicing through the bedroom's curtains. He moved his hand slowly, appreciating the man's fine asset.

The sound of Rebecca murmuring broke their concentration. Alexander turned his head, and their mouths latched greedily. So, Eric inched his way down between the man's legs and took him in his mouth. That would be enough—for now. At least it was, until Alexander pulled himself free minutes later and rolled on top of Rebecca. She let out a long moan as he entered her with a sharp pitch of his hips. If he wanted to fuck Rebecca and not Eric, then so be it. Eric had learned his lesson.

Chapter Six

ALEXANDER

Glasses clinked all around him. Voices murmured as they stood in the low-lit room. The bright lights highlighted the paintings hung on the cream-colored walls.

For the last thirty minutes, Alexander couldn't rip his gaze from the painting before him—two spread knees and what lay between them. In the picture, what he knew to be sweet, pink flesh was depicted as a flourishing garden of blues, greens, and yellows.

Another man stopped and gave him a holiday greeting that he barely heard. Alexander couldn't stop staring at the depiction of Rebecca, open, vulnerable, beautiful. Finally, the man left Alexander alone again to drink in the sight of his love.

Someone else stopped. Cleared his throat. "What do you think?"

He twisted to face Eric, his blond hair haloed by the twinkling Christmas lights of the tree behind him. Sucking in a long breath, he widened his stance. "Beautiful. Except Rebecca is a natural redhead, so the garden is a bit …"

"Lush?" Eric stepped forward, and the two men faced the painting. "It's metaphorical."

"Hmmm. Yes, and apropos, I suppose." Rebecca was the most alive person he'd ever met—besides Eric. The man had no idea how gorgeous he was. Alexander tilted his head toward the frame. "I see someone's already bought it."

"I'm surprised you were willing to auction it off, actually." Eric lifted a wine glass to his lips.

Alexander glanced at him. "Oh? I rather like your and Rebecca's idea to open that training camp. And raising funds this way. Let people have some ownership around its success." The art gallery had jumped at the chance to showcase and sell art from Alexander's private collection— and the few originals painted by Eric.

Eric's eyebrows shot up. "But not too much ownership?"

Alexander chuckled. "Maybe I've softened in my old age."

"God, let's hope not." He cleared his throat again and shuffled on his feet a bit. "What do you think of the … other painting?"

Alexander had been waiting for the question all night. He squared himself to a very nervous-looking Eric. "Which other painting?" Alexander couldn't help but tease the man. Eric was a naturally gifted painter, something he'd not shared with anyone until very recently. And the painting he'd done of Alexander was stunning.

A twinkle shone in Eric's eyes. "That one." He lifted his chin toward the portrait of Alexander.

Alexander glanced at it, once more appreciating the depiction of himself. It showed him standing in the middle of the Library, his eyes not focused on any particular scene that unfolded around him. At least, that was what a casual observer might see. On closer inspection, Alexander finally understood exactly where his eyes in the painting landed.

It didn't rest on the woman strapped to a black padded bench before him or the two men intertwined with one holding the other's head back by fistfuls of hair to the side, something Eric particularly enjoyed when Alexander did it to him.

Rather, Alexander's gaze was firmly locked on someone across the room, a woman with red hair blowing in an unseen breeze from an open window. *Rebecca.*

And in the far right corner of the painting? A blond man's reflection in an old-fashioned stand-up, full-length mirror. *Eric.* He also stared at Rebecca but held something in his hand. It took a full forty-five minutes of staring at it for Alexander to recognize the object held by Eric's depiction in the painting, as the image of him was purposefully painted half hidden from view.

It was the Contessa, Alexander's oldest flogger from a time long ago when he and Rebecca first started in the lifestyle. He'd used it on her—and Charles, their late lover. But never Eric.

The message the image gave was both hidden and clear.

Eric still felt outside after all this time.

Even after wearing Alexander's bracelet, a collar of his choice, Eric remained unsure of his place with them—as if the past was always still a ghost in a mirror.

Could he blame him? He'd been so absent of late. Then that scene before those newcomers? It had to go that way, but it wasn't right. They'd never spoken much about it afterward. Rather, swept that day under the rug.

But now, things had to change. Little did Eric know tonight was pivotal for them both in so many ways. He'd prove it … later.

Alexander had a surprise for him, and he only hoped Eric would finally understand. Alexander had disappointed him this last month or so. Not a state he entertained ever. So, tonight, the man was always free to leave. If he did, Alexander would mourn him as strongly as he had Charles.

Eric smiled at him. "The one of the old man. What do you think?"

Alexander arched an eyebrow. "I'd say the subject of the painting is still able to stuff that younger mouth of yours with something that will make you rethink your ageism."

Eric swallowed. "No ageism. Wouldn't dream of it, but if you feel the need to prove it, I—"

A light hand fell on his shoulder, and Rebecca's face appeared between them. "What are you two whispering about?"

"You," Eric said quickly.

So, Eric believed he'd dodged a bullet—or a mouth full of cock. They would both love it, of course.

"Oh, good, and … look. It sold." She pointed at the

portrait of her. "I wonder who bought it?" She craned her neck around the small crowd gathered before black onyx sculptures of bodies intertwined and abstract paintings, one depicting a woman holding a man and the other a tamer pastoral scene.

"It was sold to someone very lucky." Alexander circled her waist and drew her into him. Now that people in the room knew Rebecca had sat for the painting, too many eyes assessed her. Probably wanting to know if she was a "real" redhead since the picture gave no clue.

Still, he liked Eric's interpretation. Rebecca was similar to a lush garden. Full of quiet energy and endless surprises. He also enjoyed Eric's depiction of him. It was real.

Eric's eyes drifted down to Alexander's hold on Rebecca, then shot back up to his face. The man's thick bracelet declaring him tethered to Alexander and Rebecca was visible. Eric's fingers touched it. Instead of comfort, however, Alexander caught a flash of discontent crossing his eyes.

Alexander gestured to Eric to draw closer. "Why don't we adjourn to the back showing room? I have a surprise." He lifted his chin at Marta, the gallery owner hovering nearby. He'd asked her to stay on standby for his signal.

She nodded her head once, then moved toward them.

Rebecca twisted in his hold and gazed up at him. "There's a back room? Will there be wine? Please tell me there will be wine." He hadn't let her have any until she gained permission. It was a little game they liked to play. She couldn't drink until he did.

"Private bar, too." He led the two of them past Rebecca's

portrait. Marta would know what to do next—bring the portraits of Rebecca and him to the back room.

After getting Rebecca her glass of chardonnay and Eric an excellent malbec, Alexander moved to the back wall, where a single painting stood on an easel shrouded in a gold swath of fabric. Two empty easels bracketed the hidden picture.

He taken one sip of his wine when Marta and her team, two men dressed entirely in black, entered. Each man carried a painting. They set them up on the two waiting easels.

Eric threw him a puzzled look. "What have we here?" He then glanced at an equally puzzled looking Rebecca, who shrugged.

After Marta and the two men strode out without so much as a backward glance, Alexander moved to the shrouded painting. "I have a present for us." His hand reached for the fabric, but then he thought better of it. The moment would be pivotal.

Then again, so many moments in his life had proven so.

"Everything okay?" Rebecca's hand fell to his arm. Perhaps he had frozen for a moment. Unlike him. Hesitation was for fools. The night had to go right, however.

"Fine." He took her hand and gestured for Eric to come closer. He clasped the man's forearm and lifted Rebecca's hand to his lips. She graced him with a small, shy smile.

"Nothing's wrong, you two. Let's just say I haven't been this happy in so long. It's taking longer to get used to than I thought." He sucked in a long breath and let it out as he drank in Eric's hazel-green eyes. "I have a Christmas wish."

"You got it," Eric said quickly.

"Anything," Rebecca answered.

He dropped his hold on them and unveiled the painting with a rather dramatic yank of the fabric so it fell to the ground. Eric's mouth slowly dropped open while Rebecca stilled, though he saw her throat bob in a delicate swallow.

"This"—Alexander stepped backward—"is what I want." He lifted a hand toward the painting. "I want all three of these scenes. I've had the first two. Now, I want this third one." He pointed to the middle painting he'd just unveiled.

As Eric had worked on the portrait of him, Alexander had commissioned another painter—Francisco Sanchez, whose last portrait sold for over $100,000 in a bidding war. When Alexander, who'd funded his early days as a painter, requested a specific scene, the man had generously obliged.

"It's ..." Rebecca began. She wisely stopped. Rather, she dipped her head and stepped backward, leaving Alexander and Eric standing before it. She always had a sixth sense about things.

Eric swallowed slowly. "I don't know what to say."

"Say anything. Or don't." Alexander shrugged. "But it's what I want."

Eric stepped a little closer and bent forward to get a closer look. The request Alexander had made of Francisco was simple. Paint him dominating Eric in a scene—but not just getting to the pain-pleasure mix. Rather, capture—if he could—how Alexander felt about the great honor of lording over the man.

In the picture, Alexander's back was to the viewer. But he could be seen in that same full-length mirror as in

Eric's portrait. His eyes were cast down on a kneeling Eric. Intense. Unwavering.

Eric's face was tilted upward. He wore nothing but a lattice of ropes, his blond hair tousled as if it'd been fisted and yanked. It had been. The vision of the afternoon in the Library, when Francisco came by to do his early sketches, rushed back to Alexander's mind like a flood. He'd been brutal on the man, but he had to have full control of every second for the two newbies that day. If they thought they could take an inch and turn it into a mile at his club, they'd be sorely mistaken. Eric had played his part beautifully. But it had cost them both.

The painting captured a rare scene with just him and Eric. He couldn't even recall where Rebecca had been that day. But it was all right. He wasn't concerned about his memory or the fact that he couldn't pinpoint Rebecca's location that night. She would always be safe so long as he lived. And she would always be his true love. But Alexander had found himself enthralled with Eric that day. And many others, if truth be told.

The only difference in the painting from that scene was that Alexander held the Contessa, an instrument he'd never used on Eric before. He wanted the message to be clear. His dominance—and love—belonged to both of them. Not just one.

Francisco captured their dynamic that evening perfectly. The painting showed every tense muscle under Alexander's white dress shirt leaning toward Eric. His eyes honed in on the man kneeling before him as if he were prey and prize. Because that was what Eric was to him at that moment.

Eric hadn't moved from his stance by the painting, except for his eyes, which darted around as if searching for any message in the painting that wasn't exactly what Alexander had intended. He could search all he wanted. The picture perfectly captured who Eric was to Alexander.

Equal to Rebecca.

Alexander was the first to break the silence. "Do you understand now?"

Eric straightened and turned to Alexander. His eyes shone in the low lighting. "I think so."

"I didn't take you during that scene because you are mine and mine alone. No witnesses get to see the full story. And …"

He moved closer to Eric. "Rebecca, come here." She did as asked and nestled into his side. "I need you to understand without a doubt"—he quickly glanced at the painting and back to Eric—"you are mine and Rebecca's. Forever and as long as you wish it. You needn't ever question it again." He then leaned down, picked up a gift bag, and held it out to him.

Eric cocked his head as if he didn't understand, but he took it and peered inside. He swallowed, reached in, and pulled out the Contessa. She'd seen better days. The leather was now cracked in places, the handle frayed. "This is …" He looked up at Alexander.

"For our next scene. Only this time"—he leaned forward—"you're not getting away with just a butt plug. Understand?" He would fuck the man senseless.

Eric chuckled a little and tugged at his hair. "Sounds like I'm getting my wish instead of you." Was he attempting to lighten things?

Alexander's jaw tensed. "No. It's my wish. And every time you think yourself unequal, it …" Damn, stupid emotion lodged in this throat. Unexpected. Unwanted. He needed Eric to get it.

Rebecca's lungs expanded into his chest as she took a long breath. "It hurts," she filled in for him.

Eric's eyes widened slightly. "I would never hurt you."

"Then know what I say," he said.

Eric's shoulder's dropped an inch, and he nodded.

Alexander drew closer to him, taking Rebecca with him. 'If you ever feel that old insecurity creeping up on you, you tell me." He glanced at the portrait again. "I'll remind you."

One side of Eric's mouth inched up in his signature smirk. But he nodded. Finally, perhaps, the man got what he meant to him.

"But this time with my cock, not a butt plug." He arched an eyebrow in warning.

"Ready when you are."

Alexander chuckled. "Now, let's join the party out there." He gestured for them to move toward the door.

"But won't the owners want their two paintings? They both sold, right?" Rebecca craned her neck backward at the three paintings.

"Yes, I do want them. I own all three."

She playfully slapped his chest. "And here I thought my portrait was ending up over Seamus's mantle. He was teasing me about it all night."

"Over my dead body," Alexander said. "They're officially for our eyes only. Our secret. I hope you don't mind, especially about your work." He slapped Eric on the shoulder. "It's just I'm rather possessive over you … and Rebecca."

Lines around Eric's eyes softened. "I'm touched. Honored." He cleared his throat.

"Good. Because I plan on doing much touching tonight."

"Anything you wish," Eric said.

Rebecca nodded vigorously.

"Now"—Alexander winked at her—"before we abandon the party, care to help me with something?"

"Of course," she said.

"We're going to announce to everyone your training camp idea. Only I think we need to expand the idea. To a real school."

Rebecca clapped her hands in glee. "Perfect. And I have another idea."

Of course, she did.

"You have the Dominant's council with the Tribunal. But what if I start a submissive council?"

Eric snorted. "Are you kidding? Can you see a bunch of submissives trying to decide something? '*You ask him. No, you ask him.*'"

Alexander laughed. "You do have a point there." Sobering, he said, "But I'll consider it. I'm in a generous mood."

"Wow, remind me to ask you for a yacht," Eric said.

"We already have one." His hand steered Eric down the hallway. "Marta will wrap up all three of the paintings. They'll hang in our bedroom. In the meantime, the school starts tonight by helping Master R with Lina."

The man chuckled. "What did she do this time?" Lina's brat reputation proceeded her.

"Apparently, she's not yet learned all she needs to. Care to help?"

He shrugged. "What do you want me to do?"

"Everything. With me."

Now he got a real smile out of Eric—and Rebecca.

Alexander still knew he would have to spend the rest of his life making sure they understood it.

So, he would. Nothing he had to do for either of them would be a hardship. They were part of his soul.

Note from Elizabeth: I was promptly kicked out of the scene. *They got busy.* Imagine that.

If you'd like to read more about Alexander, Rebecca and Eric's polyamorous relationship, read **Invincible**, an Elite Doms of Washington full-length erotic romance. which you can find at your favorite online retailer or request it from your library

For more about what happens at Club Accendos, check out Elizabeth's other books by visiting www. EliabethSaFleur.com or join her email newsletter, News From Elizabeth.

When Darkness Calls

Chapter One

Charlotte placed her hand on the door. The bathroom's cold tile floor bit into her knees and bruised the tops of her feet. But the hurt was good. It helped to lift another layer of the fog that swamped her mind.

Richard's deep, rich, baritone voice reached her next. It shimmered through her whole body like she was a tuning fork he'd plucked it.

She pressed her cheek to the door and hummed the melody with him, clinging to the song's notes like a life raft. Her collar, a thin band of silver around her neck, picked up on her throat's vibration. She touched the metal, her collar, *his* collar. Forever, he'd said when he'd placed it around her neck during the ceremony. How long ago? A year.

Through the wooden door, his sharp inhale signaled he would start the song again. How many times had he run through the tune? He would keep it up for hours if she needed it.

She was so tired of needing it.

Her voice didn't come back to her at first. She cleared her throat and found some words. "My name is Charlotte. I'm in your bathroom."

"Our bathroom, love." Richard's voice was low and calm. He returned to humming the soothing melody.

"Yes, our bathroom." The door was warm from absorbing her body heat and tears over the last few minutes or hours—who could remember time? The floor was slick from her hands and damp from her sobs. The body was remarkable that way, crying pints of fluid until you had to wonder where it all came from.

Tu sie il mio sole

Il mio unico sole

The lyrics crystallized in her mind like flashes of light in a dark room. "You make me happy when skies are gray," she croaked back.

Her fingertip traced a seam in the door, hidden from the eye by layers of paint. Up close, she could see the small imperfection. She'd painted the door a sunny yellow when she'd first moved in. "Any color you'd like, love," he'd said. So, she'd covered up the former dusty blue with proverbial sunshine.

The last remnants of her dream drifted from her consciousness, and she could finally slip the horrid images into the slot in her mind she'd created for those awful memories. She pushed herself upright. She'd had a nightmare, that was all. She'd found her way into the bathroom and locked the door as if that would keep the imaginary mob from finding her.

Non lo saprai mai caro

His voice lifted into the higher notes, and a new shiver ran through her body. *You'll never know, dear.* The Italian version of the song didn't quite fit. But Richard made them fit anyway.

Everything about him fit—especially her.

"Master."

The song abruptly ended. "Charlotte."

"I'm fine." Her voice was too thin. Then again, it was three o'clock in the morning.

"Yes, you are."

He wasn't talking down to her. He was telling her exactly where to go in her mind. She obeyed. She was home. *Safe.* She reached up and unlocked the bathroom door.

Richard sat on the carpet outside, his legs drawn up, his arms casually hooked over his knees as if he sat in front of a campfire and not on their bedroom carpet, singing her off the ledge for the hundredth time since they'd moved in together.

He didn't move forward but waited. She did what she always did on nights like those. She crawled toward him and laid her cheek against his muscled thigh. "Master." She'd need to say his name like that for a while to bring herself back completely.

His hand descended on my hair and stroked. "Another one. Yet, you didn't seek me out."

"I'm sorry." The dreams were becoming more frequent now, every other night instead of every other week.

She'd find herself lying on the cold tile behind the

locked door. Someone like her could find a room with a door with a lock in their sleep. She'd learned that as soon as she'd learned to run as a child.

"I'm sorry," she repeated, not quite sure what else to say. He had to be getting so sick of her stress nightmares. If she didn't get a grip, he could leave her. Most men would have been done with her long ago.

"You're worried about today."

It was today already? The day she'd been waiting for. To walk down a runway wearing Laurent's new wedding dress design, a dress he'd spent hours fitting her into.

She loved being seen, showing herself off. So, why did she dread today? The second she was asked to do it, a thick, gray mist began to rise in her. She'd wanted to say no. But she never could say no to a dominant's request, and Sarah was one powerful Domme—not to mention Washington, DC's, most prominent stylist.

When Sarah asked her to be in the runway show, Charlotte had merely cast her eyes down and nodded. After lifting her lashes, the pleasure that spread across Sarah's eyes bloomed in Charlotte's chest, hitting her like a drug. She still thought to back out, but she killed any thought of that when Richard's face lit with delight after hearing she would show off the custom-made gown to the city's elite. After all, he'd wanted to see her in a wedding dress for so long, preferably walking toward him.

Charlotte couldn't figure out why she was so terrified of going through the fashion show and had so many nightmares about the idea. At least, she thought that was where they came from. Her memories of weddings always led to one thing: whoever her mother had married, he'd eventually made his way to her—or tried to, anyway.

It was no wonder the dreams were the same every night. She was in Laurent's dress and running from a mob of men, their black silhouettes grotesque and misshapen. Her feet bled from running—so much running. The dress was ruined with mud and dirt and torn from tripping every few steps.

Even now, safely nestled against Richard, she could call up how the white silk was nothing but shreds of fabric, destroyed from tangling among branches and brambles as she clawed her way out.

Large gashes in the long white gown showed her bare waist, and the hemline, tattered beyond recognition, bared her legs.

But it was the veil, the gossamer slip of fairy fabric, as she'd dubbed the material upon seeing it for the first time, that sent her blood thrashing in her veins.

She'd rise from falling and start running again, but the veil would snag on a tall branch she tried to duck under. The pull on her scalp was excruciating. She twisted to catch even a little bit of the tulle floating in the foggy air, but she always missed because *they* were getting closer.

In a way, her nightmare was such a cliché.

"Eyes," Richard whispered.

She raised her gaze to his and focused her attention on his face, his beautiful dark eyes like liquid obsidian.

His fingertip lifted her chin an inch. "You won't do the show."

Her spine straightened. "No. I mean, please. I want to." She'd spent countless hours preparing for the day, practicing walking and going through so many fittings. And he'd looked so proud during the first one, pleased Laurent had chosen a sheer lace for the cap sleeves and a deep V neckline for the dress. He'd remarked on it as if he'd already pictured her wearing a wedding dress.

His hand circled her neck. "Truth."

His move made her pussy instantly weep with wanting him. Any touch of his elicited such a reaction. "Always, Master."

"You don't want to do this, do you?"

She curled up in his lap instead of voicing the only thing her mind conjured up. *I want to do it for you.*

He sighed and rose. "Take off your t-shirt. Get in the shower. You will think about answering me honestly."

He pulled her to standing and led her into the bathroom, where he started the shower. She jerked her t-shirt off and stepped under the warming water. Shivered a little from it not being quite hot enough. A punishment, perhaps?

"Face the wall. Hands on the tile, legs apart. Then think about what I asked you."

She turned and did what he asked. Except for having to tell him how much showing herself off in a wedding dress scared her—and she had no idea why. She wanted to bind herself to Richard in every way possible. Collared, married, if she could slip inside his skin, she'd do it. Yet, somehow, she kept hesitating to nail down a date. Something felt … unfinished.

Fabric rustled behind her. Then the trajectory of the water raining down on her changed. He'd stepped into the shower with her.

The slap on her ass was unexpected, yet not. "Thought enough yet?"

"Yes, sir."

"You know what happens when you lie to me." He rained hard whacks to her behind until she lost all sense of the water sluicing down her body. Her whole being focused on the fire rising on her ass. Her forehead rested on the tile, moans freely rising in her throat.

The heat and sting from his slaps raised a curious hope in her. Her lower back arched as her body ached for him to continue. She'd been here so many times—with Richard, with others before him. What lay on the other side of the pain was peace.

It'd always been that way with her. The rougher someone was, the more silence lay on the other side. And Richard knew that when she was wound up, scared, coming down from nightmares she couldn't explain, she would find the words he *desperately* wanted from her only if she found that stillness inside her.

Desperately? No, he was never in that state. That was her domain.

He pressed his body against hers, his hard erection pressing into her back. "Tell me. Tell me everything."

"I'm scared, and I don't know why."

His hand curled around her throat, her collar pressing into her skin. "Of me? Or this?"

Her head turned, her cheek meeting tile. "Never. I need you. This. I just don't …"

"Don't what, il mio tesoro?"

How could he treasure her when she didn't feel she

even had her own mind? "I don't know what the truth is."

A deep, rich murmur reverberated through her back. "Ah." He spun her, her bruised ass meeting the slick tile. "Finally." His finger traced down her cheek. "Now, we're getting somewhere."

His hands moved down her neck and shoulder to cup a breast as his thumb roughly swiped across her nipple. She gasped, a trickle of arousal slipping down her inner thigh despite the water hitting her side.

One side of his mouth tilted. Then his hand moved to cup her ass. With the other, he yanked one of her legs to curl around his leg. With a bend of his knees, he then lifted her up. Richard was a tall man. She often forgot his strength despite the muscles usually on display in his arms. He was so gentle with her.

At least until he wasn't.

He pressed a kiss into her neck. "Now, feel me as I take you. Then, find the words."

His thrust inside her was swift, brutal, and she'd have it no other way.

She let herself go soft, let herself get lost again. Only this type of lost was nothing but bliss.

"Who do you belong to?" he growled as his thrusts grew longer, harder.

She clutched at his back. "You."

"And what does that mean?"

"You'll always protect me."

Then, he pitched into her as far as he'd ever gone. A cry left her throat as her nails dug into his skin. She wanted more, *needed* more.

Then, maybe, she'd find the right words. She prayed she'd never have to utter certain ones, however. Like that her fear came from knowing he couldn't protect her from everything. He couldn't protect her from her own mind.

Chapter Two

She watched him from the doorway. Richard didn't need to glance over his shoulder to know she stood there.

The slightest rush of her breath, the rustle of her skin as she twisted her fingers—all things he could pick out over a jet engine if needed. His ears were so attuned to her.

He kept his gaze on the turkey sausage sizzling in the pan. "Hungry?"

"One of these days, I'll be able to sneak up on you." She sidled up to him. "Smells good."

Liar. Slowly, she was getting used to healthier eating. None of that crap she grew up with. Food that only came from a can or the frozen section. Still, she'd eat potato chips for breakfast if left to her own device. He'd let the slight white lie—"smells good"—slide. She'd had a rough night—again.

Her wet hair hung loose around her shoulders and soaked her T-shirt. It was actually his. The old T-shirt looked better on her, hanging on her body in the most delicious way. Nipples poked through the thin cotton, and the hemline skimmed the top of her thighs, threatening to reveal her beautiful pussy lightly dusted with copper-colored hair.

He speared one of the turkey sausages with a fork and laid it on a paper towel on the counter. A greasy stain immediately fanned on the paper.

She perched herself up on the countertop and swung her bare legs.

"Does that granite feel good on your ass?" he asked.

Her eyes grew wide as she slowly slid off the countertop and leaned against it. "Sorry."

"It was an honest question." He flipped the sausage so the grease could be absorbed on the other side. He speared it once more and held it out to her.

She took it between two fingers, a slight smile crossing her face. "Yes, and thank you."

As she nibbled on her sausage, he plated the rest of the food. Scrambled eggs, wheat toast with butter and honey, and more of the sausage. She followed him to the table and nervously fidgeted as she settled herself onto the farmhouse chair.

"Still nervous about today." He didn't pose it as a question.

She nodded. "I don't know why. It's not like anyone expects me to be a supermodel."

They were there again. He had to once again prove how beautiful he found her. Shaking one's upbringing, especially one like Charlotte's, full of putdowns and snarky comments about her looks by her jealous—and often drunk—mother, was difficult. Unfortunately, hers was made worse by the stepfathers, drunken uncles, and neighborhood boys.

Then to find a good man in Daniel, marry him and have him taken away so soon? Her insecurity over having anyone good in her life was understandable.

He snapped his napkin into place. "You already rival them. Now, eat. Then, we go."

She swallowed hard but obeyed, choking down half the breakfast. Her nerves didn't settle one bit. He knew what he'd have to do.

He and Charlotte had been together for over a year. The first time he'd laid eyes on her, across the Library at Club Accendos, an uncanny love had burst through his veins like fire. He was captivated, wholly and irrevocably, by her sweetness, her needs. One introduction and it was like two magnets made only for one another clapped together, fitting as if they'd once been whole and had been split apart. He'd do anything for Charlotte—even push her when needed. He'd never again see her suffer so long as he took a breath. And her mind was turning on her.

But perhaps he'd expected too much from her over the last few months. Doubt wasn't his strong suit, but he was running out of ideas to get her over the last remnants of her anxieties. A fashion show—something that should have delighted her—should not have raised such nightmares.

Perhaps something else niggled at her consciousness, something he'd yet to unearth. Of course, he knew about her past, even if she hadn't revealed it to him herself. Someday, however, she would. He was sure of it.

She got dressed—a sundress chosen by him—and got in the car. It was hot for a late September day, and his Aston Martin's air conditioning struggled to keep up. Then again, he kept it on low for a reason. She needed him right now, and there was only one way to be there for her.

As her Master.

"Charlotte." One hand spun the steering wheel as the light turned green while his other descended on her bare thigh.

"Hmmm?" She'd been staring out the window.

His fingers dug into her flesh, and her gaze swung to him. "Are you wearing panties?"

She nodded slowly and pulled up her hemline to reveal white lace, a pair probably gifted to her by Sarah for today. "Do you want them?"

"Not yet. Open those knees wider and scoot closer."

Her lips parted in surprise, which surprised him. It wasn't as if his command was unheard of in their time together. "But—"

"Now." He slapped her leg, making her startle.

He turned onto New York Avenue. Though they might be a few minutes late to the Arts and Industries building, which Sarah had rented for the show, they'd still be early enough to score a parking space on Madison Avenue—that was, if she behaved.

The good girl opened her legs. His hand drifted on her skin for long minutes as they crawled down the street with the traffic. "Eyes forward," he instructed.

Her teeth grasped her bottom lip, and she stared out at

the windshield. He did the same.

Her chest began to rise and fall. Anticipation, perhaps? Or maybe frustration that he wasn't moving his hand to where she wanted.

One of the things he loved about his Charlotte was her desire to be touched, handled. His need to top her was as strong, but he made her wait until they found themselves passing the MCI Center. Traffic slowed even more. Honking and street noises grew louder. Finally, he gave her his fingers. Slipped them higher and touched the silky fabric. She gasped at the contact.

A deep satisfaction bloomed in his chest. God, he loved her reaction to him.

He rubbed her clit, now swollen and easily found. He rubbed his middle finger up and down until he heard her breath quicken.

"Are you wet for me, Charlotte?" he asked.

She swallowed and nodded.

"Good." The National Gallery of Art came into view. His finger continued as they turned onto Constitution. He drove down the street, turned, drove around the back end of the Smithsonian, and, again, got them back on Constitution.

She stared at his profile. He didn't need more than a periphery look at her to know her eyes held questions, her lips quivering with the need to come.

"Don't," he said when her gasps became sharp—little inhales as if she were close.

"Please?"

"No."

They continued to drive around. His fingers stalled

when he thought she got close. Starting up again when she regained some composure.

After two circles around the Smithsonian's campus, her head had fallen back. Her skin flushed a beautiful glow that brought out her freckles even more. Even her thighs were pinked, growing tense as she fought to keep them still.

When her panties were so soaked that she'd surely left a wet spot on his seat, he removed his hand.

A parking space opened up on Madison. They always did eventually and were there for the taking if one exercised a little patience.

After parking, he turned off the car. With no air-conditioned air coming from the vents, the atmosphere warmed.

He turned his gaze to her as the sun streamed across her beautiful pale skin. "Now, give them to me."

People, mostly tourists, milled about the sidewalk. They might see her slipping them off, which was a bonus. Charlotte was a notorious exhibitionist, and her arriving panty-less would not be unusual. The backstage would be filled with people close to their circle. And if Sarah had her way, she'd get Laurent's ass nice and red before walking down the runway. Probably in front of everyone backstage.

She shimmied off her panties and handed them to him. They were soaked as expected.

He curled his fingers around the fabric and balled them up. "When you put on your wedding gown, you'll think of me."

"I might ruin the dress."

"Go ahead." Her mental state was far more important

than a frock. "Let your juice run down your inner thigh. Let it pool in your shoes. I'll lick it off you later. And these," he held up her soaked panties before tucking them inside his suit jacket, "stay with me. You'll see me reach in and touch them when you come close to me." He'd made sure his seat at the fashion show was at the end of the runway. "With every step, you'll think about my fingers inside you." He thrust his hand back between her legs and jabbed his index finger inside her, making her gasp. "Won't you?"

She nodded vigorously as her lips dropped open. She was calm, though her pretty mouth quivered, and her legs shook.

His hand slipped free, and he raised his fingers to her mouth. "Suck them off. Then we go." There was more to do, but he'd need an audience.

Chapter Three

Charlotte's head fell back, and she spun in a circle. Even the ceiling was interesting with its patterns and colors. "I still can't get over this place." She'd been inside the Arts and Industries building before for the fashion show rehearsal, but her mind was still filled with awe at the space.

Richard grasped her hand. "It *is* hard to believe it's so light inside." The building's exterior was mostly red brick, with some yellow, blue, and black bricks forming decorative patterns. But it appeared almost warehouse-like and sure to be dark inside.

But once through the front entrance, the building opened into a spacious, light-filled hall with hundreds of windows, soaring archways, and ornate Moorish-inspired stenciling. The structure boasted four symmetrical spacious halls laid out in a Greek Cross with a central rotunda connecting them in the middle. They were aptly titled the North, South, East, and West Halls. Any of them would make an ideal fashion runway, with the rotunda allowing for a perfect place to turn around and walk back.

"Sarah said it's perfect for Laurent's collection. She called the building "'industrial chic with both masculine and feminine elements'."

Richard laughed. "Sounds like Sarah. Come on."

He led Charlotte down the North Hall. Her sweater tapped the back of her thighs. She'd tied it around her waist to hide the wet stain caused by Richard's magic fingers.

Her gaze drifted to the marble and limestone floor. She'd yet to spot one of the famous fossils trapped in the tiles sourced long ago from a prehistoric quarry. She'd have to stop and study them another day.

The show started in two hours. Between hair and make-up and any last-minute fittings, they needed to hustle. Not to mention, she needed time to calm her body down. His hand, however, firmly gripping hers, only reminded her of what they could do, and her body responded enthusiastically. The wet between her legs threatened to chafe her inner thighs.

Had she ever been that easy? No, only for Richard.

When they'd first met at Club Accendos, he'd intimated the hell out of her. His presence filled the room. His dark eyes, which could drill into a person's soul if you gazed into them long enough, had bored into her. Yet, even then, she'd immediately known she was safe with him. Warm energy radiated from his every pore, and she soon relaxed.

Now, if only her body could get on board with the fact she was safe walking through one hundred of Washington, DC's, elite wearing the final look of Laurent's fashion show—the wedding dress.

Her sandals clicked on the floor in time with her heartbeat. Richard didn't seem hurried or concerned that his touch would continue the ache in her body or her desire for him to sweep her away into a hall closet and have his way with her again.

"What's going on in your beautiful head?" He kept his gaze locked on the rotunda ahead.

"How much fun it'd be to turn around and spend the day in bed."

He laughed. "You're taking my request for truth today seriously. Good." He finally peered down at her. "I have something better planned."

"Your better is always better." The smile crossing his face told her he was pleased with her answer. She'd meant the words.

They slowly made their way toward the makeshift dressing rooms at the end of the South Hall.

Empty of visitors, there was so much to see along the way.

Men and women in black shirts and pants sporting crisp white aprons busied themselves on either side of them. They snapped white linens into place on round tables. They unstacked tall towers of gold cane chairs and settled them around each table. A woman to her right fussed with a floral arrangement of orchids and lilies.

In a few hours, more than one hundred people would crowd the tables. Charlotte would walk down the center as patrons sipped glasses of champagne and wine and enjoyed a simple late lunch. Her runway walk would take her to the rotunda, where more people would be sitting—and watching her. She was to walk around the hexagon shape in the center that held a marble statue of Aphrodite, erected just for the show.

"Laurent is such a romantic," Richard said as they passed the statue. "I should expect a lot of lace and pink today?"

"I've only seen the wedding dress. Sarah said he wanted everything to be a surprise the day of. But she did say his collection is meant to be a reflection of the strength it takes to love and be loved." She hadn't meant to say so much about it. Richard's handling that morning must have done more to loosen her tongue than she'd realized.

She swallowed hard as they drew closer to where she'd get ready for the show. Her unwelcome nerves crawled up her legs. She buckled a little at the entrance of the North Hall.

Richard dropped his hand, and his arm was around her bicep in a nanosecond. Tension furrowed his brow, and her stomach dropped. "My body doesn't seem to get the message that everything is going to be fine," she tittered.

One side of his mouth quirked up, the lines smoothing across his forehead. "It will." His arm circled her shoulders, and they continued their advance toward the people bustling about.

"If you do exactly as I say. And remember my fingers."

A small twinge went off between her legs.

They stepped behind a fabric wall, and she stopped short. "Oh, hello." She'd have thought they'd stepped into Club Accendos if she didn't know better.

A blonde woman in nothing but a T-shirt hiked up over her back grasped two arms of a tall director's chair as a man alternatively rubbed and spanked her bare ass. Another guy was being laced into a rope corset by two other men. A woman, tall and thin, moaned off to the side as a short brunette dressed in head-to-toe velvet played with her nipple jewelry.

It was all considered fairly light play for their circle of friends. Still …

Then again, she'd signed a contract saying she'd consented to be backstage and possibly witness various forms of "warm-up play," as Sarah described it. So long as any playtime didn't interfere with the fashion show, Sarah said it was fine. Charlotte didn't believe anyone would exercise that freedom, however.

Still, good thing it would all end by the time they stepped away from the dressing area and into Washington's society audience. Not everyone understood their world. Perhaps that was the point? Play backstage while those sitting in the audience had no idea what was really going on? A reminder they were surrounded by friends?

Sarah appeared from behind one of the models, a stunning brunette with large almond-shaped eyes and generous curves. The Femme Domme rushed up to Richard and kissed him on one cheek and then the other. "Ah, you're here." She sent her dark eyes Charlotte's way.

Richard inclined his head down to Sarah, who was much shorter than him. Most people were. "I need to speak with you," he said quickly.

Her lashes flicked up, and something crossed between

them. She nodded once. A slice of curiosity ran through Charlotte, but she tamped it down. She had no reason to feel anything bad about their exchange. They were friends, after all.

Sarah smiled at her. "Charlotte, my lovely. Quickly come. Laurent's been waiting for you. Laurent!" she called out and raised her arm.

Across the room, Laurent stood, arms crossed, shaking his head as he assessed a man in an eggplant-purple sheer jumpsuit. Laurent wore a pair of chaps, his bare ass showing welts on both cheeks.

Laurent's head snapped around at Sarah's voice. It was hard to tell if the glee in his eyes came from the fact he was about to show off his fashion collection, a woman he loved called out to him, or the state of his ass. He was a notorious masochist.

There was no mistaking who caused his welts, however. One of his Dominants, Stefan, sat in a director's chair nearby looking like a Swedish god on his throne. A riding crop lay across his crossed legs.

Laurent strode up to her and Richard. In her periphery, she caught Stefan nodding once at Sarah, and she acknowledged him back. A hand-off, perhaps?

In their friends' and colleagues' circle, anything was okay so long as it followed the protocol of safety and consent. Sarah and Stefan shared Laurent—and each other—in a unique relationship.

Charlotte often envied how much they radiated the sheer *rightness* of their situation. There was no question they worked. It was the same with her and Richard—

despite their fourteen-year age difference. At least until her nightmares appeared.

A tall black man sporting gold eyeliner and the kindest smile appeared in front of Charlotte. "Ah, but first me. You must be the wedding belle. I'm Martin. Ready for your lashes?" He held up two pairs of false eyelashes pinched between his fingers.

"She is," Richard's deep voice said. "I'll be over in a second. I need to speak with Sarah and Laurent. Alone."

Now, her curiosity was piqued higher. He and Sarah turned away to talk.

Martin led Charlotte to a tall director's chair, and they went to work. "They" turned out to be Martin's team. A blonde woman named Clementine, who had the thinnest nose Charlotte had ever seen, and another very short man who simply introduced himself as "Martin's assistant extraordinaire." His job apparently was holding out makeup brushes one by one like a surgical nurse while Martin dabbed at her face with so many different shades she had no idea what she'd look like in the end.

"Such lovely skin," Martin said.

"Mmm-hhhm," his assistant agreed.

She wished she could see what they were doing. That was when it dawned on her. There were no mirrors in the entire dressing area.

A few minutes later, Richard pulled another tall director's chair beside hers. His hand possessively cupped her knee while the hair and makeup team worked her over.

"How do I look? she asked.

"Perfect." He proceeded to massage her thigh with his

hand.

"Everything okay?"

"Yes."

Okay, he wasn't going to share with her what he, Sarah, and Laurent had talked about.

While Martin continued his "magic"—as declared by his assistant every few seconds—Clementine went to work on Charlotte's hair.

First, her hair was pulled back into a series of sleek ponytails. The pulls grew stronger, and her skull stung as the woman began to intricately do … something, perhaps braided though it was something infinitely more complicated.

Charlotte's collar moved a little around her neck as the woman worked around it. It wasn't coming off ever, and it occurred to her then that she and Laurent had never spoken about it appearing in the show. Her fingers rose to touch it.

Richard's eyes slanted to her. "Good. Remember that when you walk."

"I'll try."

He faced her. "Try?"

She nodded her head vigorously. "I mean, I will."

After long minutes of being handled by so many people, a slight fog enveloped her mind, and her shoulders relaxed. The pull on her scalp, the soft dabs of the makeup brushes, and Richard's hand massaging her leg lulled her into a sort of trance.

"Relax your mouth," Martin said. As her lips fell open, Martin tapped her lips with something.

"This beigey pink is fantastic against your skin," he

declared.

"Pink does look good on her. Especially her cheeks," Richard said in a low growl.

Maybe it was her turn to have her ass turned that particular shade? She was up for it.

Finally, Martin stood back a few feet and assessed her as if a painter assessing his canvas. Richard stood up and crouched down before her.

"So, warrior or princess look?" Charlotte moved her hand to her head.

"Non," Clementine cried out in a French accent and moved Charlotte's hand back to her lap. "No touching."

Richard's hand on her knee tightened. "That's my responsibility. And privilege. And I'd say you're a warrior princess."

A small crowd began to form around them. Sarah, Steffan, Clementine, Martin, and his assistant created a half-moon circle behind Richard, who knelt before her. She wasn't used to towering above him like that.

Their faces were unreadable, which only meant one thing. Something *was* afoot.

A rustle of fabric sounded, and Clementine stepped back to let Laurent enter their circle. He held up the wedding dress she would be modeling.

Layers and layers of pale, icy blue silk dotted with seed pearls and Swarovski crystals cascaded like waves down the dress's skirt, while the top half was a tightly fitted corset. The sheer cap sleeves and deep V neckline were adorned with Swarovski crystals that twinkled in the light.

"It's more beautiful than I remembered," Charlotte said.

"Yes, beautiful," Richard whispered. He hadn't risen or peered over at the dress. His eyes remained fixed on her. "Now, open her legs more."

Richard slowly tried to part her legs. Normally, she let it happen. She loved giving him full access to her anytime he wanted. Let his hands move her body around, part her legs, do anything. It was at the crux of their relationship—fully consented to and fully understood.

But her muscles oddly fought his direction.

The answer as to why came through so clearly that she was shocked by it. *The dress had entered the room.* She almost said it aloud but knew how little sense it made. It's fabric. Thread. Crystals. Not even her dress. She'd wear it for … What? Thirty minutes? Its power over her, however, was unmistakable.

Richard yanked her up to standing, and she gasped. He spun her around and pressed his whole body against hers. Against his larger frame, she'd always felt smaller, delicate, yet oddly comforted. Right then, she wasn't sure what she felt.

He pressed her forward until she had no choice but to grasp the arms of the chair.

"For that," he growled into her ear. "You get two."

Two what? Spanks?

He kicked her legs apart. She had to scramble a little to keep herself from pitching forward into the chair. A sliver of fear she might harm her make-up or hair entered her mind but vanished when she realized a dozen people had circled them. They were watching her get a punishment.

He pushed her dress up her back, revealing her bare ass

to all. It wasn't the first time many of them had seen her in that state.

"Twenty minutes," someone called.

There was no time. What was Richard doing? How about only what she'd promised herself long ago. To be available to him. To trust him. To know whatever he chose to do would benefit her.

His hand moved slowly over the small of her back, her ass, and back up again. "It's a shame this will be covered up in … What was that?"

Sarah's voice answered. "Nineteen minutes, Master R. Make it quick."

"Ordering me?" he asked.

"Urging you on." The steel in her voice matched Richard's.

"Present." Richard's voice was as hard as she'd ever heard. She arched the small of her back and pushed her behind backward.

His fingers played along her labia, spread her flesh, and found what they sought. He thrust his index finger inside her. She was still so wet that he had no trouble slipping inside.

"You aren't ready for today, are you?"

She shook her head. "I want to be, though."

"Listen to me, Charlotte," he said low in her ear. "I know what this is. No one will get within ten feet of you in that dress or any other state without going through me. And to remind you of that fact," his fingers left her, and a small whimper left her throat at their absence, "you will take these."

Something cool and round entered her vagina. Then another. *Ben Wa balls*. And everyone saw him insert them.

His voice remained low. "Feel them. Know they're mine, and I am walking with you." Her insides flipped over. She liked the sensation of being filled with something of his.

The collar should have been enough, but now, he was *inside* her.

Richard knew what he was doing—and she shouldn't have questioned it even inside her mind. When he touched her like that, her mind went blank. Her body stilled. Her demons quieted—at least for a little while. He took her fear and overwrote it. Now, he would be touching her on the inside, through two small metal balls, for her entire walk.

He righted her and spun her around. Her dress fell to her thighs, and a trickle of juice ran down one inner thigh. Part of her hated that she cared what it'd do to the dress. The other part? An odd, almost wicked glee that it couldn't intimidate her enough to tamp down any reaction she had to her Master. Even if she wasn't worthy of its opulence.

Richard, her love, her Master, gazed down at her with his dark eyes. "Now, you're ready."

Chapter Four

Charlotte stepped from behind the black lacquer accordion divider, took two steps, and paused. Richard's heart cycled through its usual pattern upon seeing her. Like an internal storm surge, an overwhelming swell started low in his belly, then radiated outward until it threatened to break out of his chest. Love did that to a man.

His mind, however, sharpened as if he needed to stay alert to anything she needed. He grew hyper-conscious of every muscle twitch in her body, every shift in her energy.

A rough, male voice interrupted his awe of her. "She's beautiful."

Marcos Santos may be the only man alive who could say that to him and get away with it. The guy had known Charlotte longer than Richard had. Then there was the not-so-small thing of caring for her after her late husband, Daniel, died. For that, Richard would always be grateful.

The thought that she'd been out in the world alone with her past? A shudder threatened to shake him from the mere thought.

But she was better now. His ego swelled at the thought that he had something to do with it. The truth was, she was stronger than she knew, and she was about to prove it.

He sucked in a deep breath to still his over-reactive heart. "The color is stunning on her."

"Is she nervous?" Mark turned to him with worry in his eyes.

Richard had to remind himself the man was ex-special ops and Master and husband to Isabella, who was also in the show. Marcos was not competition. He was honestly worried for Charlotte. Not to mention the man was consequential in getting them together. Richard wasn't jealous.

Rather, the fact that Marcos would question her state of mind worried him. "Why do you ask?"

"Just a feeling." The man's gaze then shot forward. "There's something strange in the air. It's probably nothing. Crowds and I don't … mix."

Now, Richard was nervous. Marcos' sixth sense about these things had always proven correct. Richard glanced around quickly, but like a homing beacon, his gaze was pulled back to Charlotte.

She stood tall, shoulders back. No fear emanated from her glazed blue eyes, and a slight smile played on her lips. She began to advance, her lips parting, her fingers slightly twitching. Ah, feeling the balls inside her shift, move, reminding her of who she belongs to?

Their gazes caught. She was far away, but there was no

mistaking they locked eyes.

His goddess.

He reached into his breast pocket and touched her panties that he'd tucked away just for that moment. When he pulled his fingers out, he touched them to his lips and sent the kiss her way.

Her smile spread wider, and she let her gaze go soft as she made her way past the crowded tables.

Her steps were measured and confident. Stiff silk rustled, and the long veil affixed to her hair floated behind her as she moved as graceful as a deer tiptoeing through the woods.

Everything about her was gentle and kind. Soft. He, however, grew harder as she neared.

For a man approaching forty, he'd known many women. He'd never wanted anyone like he wanted Charlotte.

Fragile women didn't usually interest him. Yet from the first night they'd met two years ago, a frantic longing to know her, shelter her, became his mission.

It took him the better part of six months to convince Marcos—self-assigned as her temporary Master—to let him even speak to her. Marcos' fierce protectiveness had spoken volumes.

Richard could grow angry all over again if he let himself think too long about what caused her emotional scars. Stories first shared by Marcos over beers at a seedy little Irish pub on Columbia and then later by Charlotte herself. Yet she hadn't told him the whole story, had she?

From a distance, she looked as if she could break. But she never did, contrary to how her mind played tricks on her. He'd learned fast that Charlotte's vulnerabilities were not weaknesses.

She was quite formidable in her own way. Only the strongest could still love after suffering wounds such as hers.

And, God, he loved her. So, there was no question she could be okay.

Charlotte was a mere ten feet away when she hesitated and broke his gaze to look at the table behind him. Her smile froze; her breath hitched. Then, she continued forward. Anyone else would think she'd lost her footing for one brief second. Richard glanced over his shoulder at whatever made her pause.

Son of a bitch.

Richard had never told Charlotte how thoroughly he'd investigated her past. She and Marcos may have filled in certain parts, but Richard's gut told him he had more to learn. One very good private investigator later, he'd learned the truth. If he could, he'd have bleached his brain to get the disgusting images out of his head. He'd have done far more to rid Charlotte of them.

And the person responsible for the worst of it? He casually sat in an expensive gray suit, legs crossed, five feet behind him.

Wayne Trembill.

The man was the dead opposite of everything he—-and his circle—-stood for. The men and women in Richard's community did not harm. They also didn't rest until there was peace, love, and compassion in every corner of life for each other.

In that regard, Richard had come to the community fortunate. He'd learned to love women early. His mother, Italian, beautiful, and a "handful," as his father called her, ruffled his hair and pulled him in for warm hugs. Aunts and cousins all showered him with nothing but love. He'd inhaled their unique scents of Arpege, flour, and fabric softener from their cotton dresses, and it never, ever occurred to him that anyone would raise their hands or voices to those women. In his family, they never did.

But Charlotte had a very different childhood. He'd never understand how a man could toy with a woman—and Charlotte had been a spinning top in a game she'd never agreed to play for far too many years.

But then her luck changed. Her late husband had rescued her in a way. And then he'd died, but not before sealing a promise with Marcos to care for her—though, his travel schedule made it difficult to be around all the time, so …

Now, Richard was dedicated to her never needing *luck* again. Certainly not to hope or wish the arrogant bastard sitting behind him would ever show his face again.

The guy had the audacity to adjust his suit jacket and nod at Richard. Then he returned his smirk toward Charlotte, whose eyes now darted around the room. Wayne usually traveled in a pack; she thought more of them were there. Perhaps Marcos' instincts weren't so far off.

Richard's jaw would shatter in his head if he allowed that bastard—or anyone he came with—to stay in the building. Hell, in the entire city.

Marcos rose. Ah, so he'd recognized the son of a bitch,

too.

Choices ran through Richard's head. Stay seated for Charlotte—let her see he was there for her. If he rose, it might throw her off, making her mind spin about what he would do to the smug interloper.

And truth? Every fiber of his being screamed to rise and take charge.

But he stayed seated. For her.

Marcos was behind Wayne in seconds. His hand descended on the fucker's shoulder. With an offended air, Wayne rose and let Marcos lead him away.

As soon as Charlotte was out of eyesight, walking away from Richard to head back down the hall, he shot to standing. No way in hell would Marcos deal with it for him.

The men were easy to find, around the corner halfway down the East Hall. For one, Marcos was a large man with close-cropped hair and shoulders as wide as a mountain. Three more Club Accendos Dominants hovered nearby— as they would, given their bond went far beyond needing words like "I need backup." A simple nod across a room would suffice. Seeing Marcos lay a hand on a man they didn't know was all the signal they'd need to stand with him.

Wayne didn't seem to notice he was surrounded. Or rather, didn't seem to care. He should have.

Derek, whose wife Samantha was also in the show, lazily leaned against the wall with his permanent smirk that one could mistake for peacekeeping—which would be a *big* mistake. Richard had seen the guy box.

Carson, as tall and broad as Marcos, was the closest to

Wayne after Marcos. Carson's temper could ignite the walls if the guy made a wrong move. His wife, London, had her share of past abuse and was probably there. She'd likely handled the public relations for Laurent's fashion debut.

Then, there was Alexander, who, of course, wouldn't have missed Sarah or Laurent's fashion show, even if his own two loves weren't in attendance. He and Sarah had a special bond.

He was the farthest away, yet somehow, his energy filled the hall. It wasn't because he was a full six-foot-five inches tall. His commanding air would make a head of state pause and notice.

All in all, the men were a pack and as dangerous as they needed to be, especially if the women—or men—who they protected were on the premises.

Richard marched forward. "Marcos."

The man lazily turned his head to glance at him. With a quick purse of the lips and a nod, he and Carson wisely stepped backward.

"Your show," Marcos said.

Richard got within inches of Wayne's smug face. "Get out."

As usual, the bastard chuffed, followed by a quirk of his lips topping off his arrogant repertoire. "As her husband, I'd say I have every right to be here."

Chapter Five

She knew the day would come when Wayne would show up. Try to claim her once again. As if the judge's decree on their years-ago annulment meant anything to him. He was not one to follow the rules.

But did his appearance have to be today?

She'd wanted her walk to be flawless, perfect. Yet seeing him had her faltering, causing a slight pause in her advance down the catwalk. It pissed her off—until the usual terror took its place. The pattern was always the same around him. A slice of heat ran through her body, followed by a cold chill that washed over her like a tidal wave.

In her periphery, she sought Richard. He'd kept his gaze on her through her entire walk. And, as she knew it would, as soon as her hesitation took over, she felt him. His presence was like a giant invisible hand curling around her whole body, urging her forward despite her fear.

You know what? Wayne could go to hell. Even so, her renewed bravado didn't stop her from automatically searching the crowd. Wayne rarely traveled alone. His posse of idiots had to be with him.

But then again, *she* was not alone. Never would be again.

She continued walking until she got to the end of the catwalk. She rounded the corner of the tall accordion screen, and Laurent caught her in a half embrace. Her knees had given out.

Richard had always told her to "take the small victories, and they will turn into larger ones." So, she was proud of herself for waiting to crumble once out of Wayne's sight.

"I'm okay," she said automatically to Laurent. "I-I am fine. Nerves, that's all."

"Quickly. It's time for the final parade." He grasped her shoulders.

She couldn't go back out there, could she?

She had to.

She would not disappoint Laurent—or Richard.

Laurent sighed and dropped his arms. "This," he waved his hands up and down her torso. "is some of my greatest work. You're going to look gorgeous in it when you take your march down the wedding aisle. Now, go … I'll be right behind you," he whispered dramatically.

She smoothed her hands down the bodice. "It's the most gorgeous thing I'll ever wear. Thank you." *If Wayne doesn't fuck that up.*

She clasped both his wrists, and his smile returned. "Whenever you have time to make it, of course."

His brow furrowed. "Make it? Darling, it's been *made*. You're wearing your wedding gown."

Oh. "Richard bought it, didn't he?"

Laurent raised one eyebrow as if to say, "Duh."

Richard had been in a hurry to marry her a mere two months after they met. And technically, she was free to do so. If only Wayne hadn't shown up and tried to ruin it. Richard knew about her past—at least most of it, like how after Daniel died, she barely held on.

She was easy prey for Wayne and his gang. She was more than easy. She might as well have had a target on her ass.

They showed up nearly every night at the bar where she worked. At first, Wayne had been kind. Large tips left behind. Telling the other men to back off when they got drunk and their hands wandered to her butt. He started hanging out toward the end of her shift, helping her stack sticky chairs on even stickier tables. He'd walk her to her car to make sure she got there safely. At first, she'd felt protected. But then ...

Shake it off. She had a new life waiting for her. There was no reason to visit the old one.

She took a cleansing breath, then found her place in the line-up with Laurent behind her. He grasped her shoulders, squeezed once, and squealed. Before she knew it, her feet were gliding her forward with the rest of the models.

A wall of applause hit her as soon as she re-entered the South Hall. People were on their feet, clapping excitedly.

Her eyes frantically searched the crowd for Richard. He was nowhere to be found. But then again, neither was

Wayne. His minions, however, stood off to the side, like sentinels waiting for a chance to strike.

She recognized one, a tall, lanky guy she'd labeled Sneerface. He never talked much. But rather scoffed his way through most conversations. Another guy she didn't recognize stood next to him. Sneerface leaned down and whispered something to him. The man's eyes sliced her way, and he nodded once.

Shit. Were they planning to snatch her already?

Where was Richard? She had to find him. Once she was off the runway, she turned back behind the garment racks, kicked off her shoes, and slipped on her flats. Screw taking off the dress, though she itched to rip it off.

She didn't belong in a wedding dress, let alone one of Laurent's creations.

When she'd been wearing it, showing it off, she'd felt new—like clean spring rain. Seeing Wayne, his disgusted face—yes, it was pure disgust coloring his eyes—she'd curdled inside. The look was familiar. It had its usual effect. Shame tried to creep into every pore.

The stiff blue silk rustled as she scooted down the hall. The Arts and Industries building was big but not impossibly large. She had to find him—and prayed he wasn't with Wayne.

If they were together … Well, Wayne, certainly, would have nothing good to say about her. Because if she knew one thing about him, he'd ruin whatever good he saw happening around Charlotte.

Richard's low rumble echoed in the East Hall. The rich tone drew her forward like a siren's call.

She rounded the corner. Wayne was pressed against the wall. Familiar men stood around Richard, who was mere inches from him.

Sneerface strode up behind her, went around her as if she were nothing more than an obstacle to ignore, and marched up behind Richard.

Marcos' hand flew out and landed on the guy's chest. "Step back, buddy. Not your scene."

Marcos had gotten her away from Wayne—once he'd learned what had happened between them. But maybe Sneerface and Marcos had never met? Her memory around that time was spotty.

Sneerface earned his name as he leered back at Marcos. *Stupid man.* The guy was playing with fire and didn't even realize it.

She'd been so fixated on finding Richard that it was only then she realized that the other men with Marcos were Carson, Derek, and *Alexander*.

Whatever was going down was serious.

She didn't know what courage she found, but she ran up to them. "Stop," she called.

Richard's eyes turned to her, blazing with fury. "Get back to Sarah."

"No." She lifted her chin and brazened a look at Wayne. He'd aged. Lines marred his forehead, but basically, he was the same shyster. Slicked back hair. Expensive suit that he made look cheap. Why did she not see the poser he was back then?

The fire lit anew in Richard's eyes. "Now, Charlotte."

Alexander touched her elbow but said nothing.

Wayne let out a puff of air from his nostrils, screwed his lips together, and shook his head slowly. "Really, Charlotte? A wedding dress. At least you knew better than to wear white."

When she'd been walking down the catwalk, the dress had begun to feel good, like maybe she and it belonged together. It was something pretty, frail but strong, something she'd begun to feel. It was ridiculous, really. She was only one of those things. *Weak*. Easily taken in. Then used up beyond recognition. Damaged goods didn't get pretty packages like lace and silk and ...

"Alexander, please." Richard's voice ran through her like sandpaper. The fury in his eyes did more damage to her soul. She'd never be clean again because the message was clear. "Get her out of here," he said.

Alexander urged her back. "I'll escort you, Charlotte."

Sneerface, for the first time since she'd known him, actually spoke. "An escort for an escort. That's appropriate."

Richard's gaze snapped to him. "You don't say a word to her or risk losing your tongue."

Wayne looked past him and chuckled. "Oh? Didn't know that about our little redhead here? As I told you, she was no more than a prostitute when I found her." Triumph filled his eyes.

Richard's head snapped to the side, his eyes slicing over his shoulder toward her but not fully meeting her gaze. His head cocked as if he didn't understand. Then his shoulders dropped as if Wayne's words made sense. *Escort. Whore. Hooker.* Wayne had filled him in—or his version of things, anyway.

Wayne did what he'd set out to do. He'd ruined her—again.

Alexander's hold on her elbow tightened, and as if she were trash, he took her out of the hall and steered her back to the South Hall.

Alexander didn't say a word until they rounded the corner. Then he stopped her abruptly and looked down at her with those ice-blue eyes. "Do not let them get to you."

His voice was so commanding that, under normal circumstances, she might consider what he said.

"What were they talking about before I got there? I mean, they didn't …" She almost asked it out loud. Alexander had that effect on people. He often had them admit things, tell the truth.

Truth.

Richard had asked for that, hadn't he? Only there was one truth he would never forgive her for, and it would end everything. How badly she'd *let* him use her.

How Wayne coerced her into marrying him.

How he, at first, made love to her sweetly.

How it had turned ugly.

How he never took "no" for an answer.

How he was the one who turned her into a prostitute.

He once locked her out of the car in a parking lot in the pouring rain until she promised to give him a blow job. Eventually, he didn't allow her food unless she gave him sexual favors.

Her ribs hurt from hunching over. "I just need to get out of here. Could you drive me to …?" She almost said "home," but she wasn't sure she'd have one again.

"Richard will want to drive you home," he finished.

"I can't stay here."

"You must."

Then she had to get out of the wedding dress right now. She rushed forward, went behind the curtain, and started ripping at the dress.

"Whoa, there, you're going to ruin it," one of the dressers cried. He started to help her out of it, but she couldn't get it off fast enough.

Sarah rushed over with Laurent. "Charlotte, what's going on?"

Richard's voice met her ears. "Give us a minute."

Like a receding wave on a beach, everyone slunk back.

Richard's face morphed into something she couldn't read. She'd thought she'd memorized all his faces, but right then, his face wasn't recognizable in the slightest—tense lips, eyes hooded with fury.

That was the moment, wasn't it? When her life fell apart again?

Richard strode up to her and peered down at her. "I'll take her out of the dress."

Of course, he would. He'd never want to see it on her again.

A while ago, Richard had told her about his grandmother Maria. How she'd had to do whatever it took to survive Mussolini's terror in Sorrento—even using her own body. How she'd vowed never to be at the mercy of men again and made everyone in their family swear to pass on a promise: never let another woman in their family stoop so low.

Richard's mother had made him promise the same

thing. To never let a woman in his path bring herself to his grandmother's state—to let herself be taken to the point of sacrificing one's own dignity.

Charlotte had always felt somehow that meeting Richard was kismet, a sign from his mother's grave.

But now? He'd learned the worst of her, and his anger, shining from his eyes, made her skin prickle.

He took her back to the farthest corner of the dressing area and pulled her behind one of the accordion screens. He spun her so she faced away from him. Then silently began to unbutton the tiny row of buttons down her back. He wasn't gentle.

"Spread your legs. There's something of mine I'm going to retrieve," he growled.

Ah, the Ben Wa balls. She'd nearly forgotten they were there. He removed them, letting them clatter to the floor.

She leaned her forehead on her forearms against the wall and gave up. She began to weep.

He pressed against her. "You will never see them again."

She nodded and sniffed. "And you?"

His hands fell to her shoulders, and he sighed heavily. Then he spun her around. The dress was fully unbuttoned, and the bodice dropped her waist. She automatically folded her arms over her breasts. They were covered in tiny pasties but still. She'd never felt so exposed in her life.

His dark eyes had softened. "Charlotte, do not hide yourself."

Her eyes glanced around. There were just a few people milling around. Everyone else had probably moved on to the after-party by then.

"I'm … I'm …" she kept saying.

"You're what, Charlotte? A victim of a man who made you feel you deserved his treatment of you? How he labeled you something that you didn't choose to be."

"What?"

"You don't think I didn't look into every corner of your life? Let the dress fall to the ground. You are more important."

She did what he asked, and the silk pooled around her calves, the stiff skirt not letting it collapse entirely.

She stood there nude, exposed.

He sighed heavily. "I've been watching Wayne and his posse for some time. I see how he treats women. How he makes them feel."

"Like a prostitute," she whispered.

"But you aren't. If anything, he is. He can't live without manipulating someone. He traded his life, his morals, his very soul in order to get his fix. I'd say that makes him the prostitute—though it would be an affront to all legal sex workers to put him in their camp."

Richard could never fault anyone for their choices so long as there was consent.

He drew her to him, and his fingers traced along the seam of her bare ass. "Now, who are you?"

"Charlotte."

"And?"

"Other than that, I don't know."

"Then I'll remind you. Widen those legs."

He had to be kidding. "People will see." Though whatever he did to her now, most of the people still lingering backstage had already witnessed at Club Accendos.

"Charlotte. Now."

Chapter Six

Violence ran deep in Richard's blood. God, he prayed, let it be temporary. If his hands weren't full of Charlotte's red hair, now tumbled free of its braids and pins, he might have acted on the rivers of rage running through his veins. He'd spin on his heel, go back to Wayne, and rid himself of it—through his fists.

But anger was the last thing Charlotte needed from him.

Richard had to steel his throat just to soften his voice. "Shhh, baby." He tightened his grip on her hair and exposed her long, pale neck. "I know exactly what you need."

Her eyes darted around his face as if searching. "But—"

His tongue swiped over her bottom lip, the taste of her so familiar and sweet. "Marcos is handling them."

They—as in Wayne and his two lapdogs—didn't stand a chance against Marcos. The man wasn't just muscle. He knew how to rid someone for good if required. All legal, of course, though, given the anger boiling under Richard's skin, he didn't care if Marcos broke every law on the books.

Charlotte's gaze darted over his shoulder and widened. She squinched her eyes closed when the shuffle of men's feet behind him stopped. He didn't need to turn around to know Carson, Derek, and Alexander had strode up behind him.

When Richard had asked the other men to join him, his plan was crystal clear. Now, seeing fear in her eyes, he second-guessed himself. It wasn't a usual state for him. But if he knew one thing, Charlotte's dreams would return in force now and needed advanced handling. The only way to truly rid Charlotte of them was to flip the script.

He rid her of the wedding dress, kicking it to the side, not giving a shit about it at the moment. Fabric rustled by their feet, the dress likely being dragged away by Sarah. He'd enlisted her help along with the others.

Charlotte's hair hung messily over her forehead, her lips already bruised from his passionate kisses.

"Open your eyes," he ordered.

She dragged her eyes open. So many emotions warred in all that blue. Relief, passion, fear.

But moments like those were his element. Bringing Charlotte back from the brink, as harshly as required, was his forte. His goal grew larger. He would bring her back for good.

His hand cupped hers. "You're worried."

She nodded slowly.

"That's an affront to me. An affront to everyone who loves you standing behind me."

She blinked, her lips parting. "I didn't mean—"

"Didn't mean what? You think someone as small as Wayne Trembill could ever do anything to you again?" Or *any* man who wasn't Richard, for that matter? As if any of their Accendos family would allow such a thing.

He pressed his crotch against hers, instantly thickening on contact. A wave of need swept through him like wildfire, his cock hardening and pressing against his zipper. Her brilliant blue eyes sparked.

The chemistry between them was undeniable. They hadn't even started, and already, he could unload in his pants like a teenager dry-humping in a backseat. However, years of disciplining his body made that possibility as remote as Wayne ever getting to rest his eyes on Charlotte again. Never mind the guy's hands.

Richard cupped her face. "You are mine. And only mine." His gaze dropped quickly to her throat, to the circle of silver that told the world Charlotte was his.

"Yes, Master." Her lids dropped.

Acquiescing? Responding with a rote honorific? That's not what he wanted or needed. Not what *she* needed.

He finally admitted something that had niggled at the edges of his mind for months. She didn't fully believe she was safe. Years of being terrorized by others had etched into her bones. And he'd had enough of it.

"Master?" His hand trailed down her back and cupped her beautiful bottom. His finger found what it sought. He thrust one finger inside her ass, and she gasped into his mouth. "Then, should I fuck you here? In front of everyone? Or …" His other hand reached down her front, his middle and forefingers spreading her pussy lips open. "Or here?"

Her mouth dropped open, but she didn't answer. He thrust his fingers inside her pussy. Now speared with both hands, her legs began to tremble. Her arousal was clear, however, by how wet she grew.

"I don't think I can. Any of it," she blurted out.

Ah, truth. "You have a safe word."

She shook her head vehemently.

"Or is it because you don't believe I'd take care of you? Or because you're not ready to let go of your fear?" Perhaps she believed it defined her. Kept him around. Made him prove time and again that he would always be there for her. Or she didn't know who else to be.

"I'll disappoint you," she said quickly. "That's what I thought today. In the show, in … everything. And it hurts knowing I'll …"

Ah, Wayne's final lesson. No matter how hard she'd tried to please him, it had not been enough. "Fail? That's for me to decide. You don't get to predetermine that."

He withdrew his fingers. Her legs instantly relaxed, and she sunk against the wall. He pinched one of her nipples, and she cried out.

"Hurt?"

She nodded.

"I feel your pain. Always. You know that?"

Her chin wobbled, a sheen of tears forming in her eyes.

He twisted her other nipple, and she winced. "Do you?"

"Y-yes, sir." She blinked at him, a single tear escaping her sad eyes.

"Then, give it to me. All of it. It's my pain now. Not yours."

A stuttered breath left her throat. "I don't want you to have it. No one should."

Finally, an opening. "Tell me again. What is the worst thing he ever did to you?"

She shuddered from head to toe. "You know," she whined.

He did. How he'd handed her over to other men to be toyed with, played with. Then told her she didn't deserve *them*. What a crock of psychological shit.

And it'd all been recorded. He'd never told her he'd seen the video evidence—grainy footage taken on an early iPad. A device and the ensuing recordings he constantly had to force himself to remember had been thoroughly destroyed by Marcos last year. But it appeared images from one's own mind didn't fade so easily.

Richard captured her lips with his own. No more words. He kissed her gently until that tiny rumble in the back of her throat sounded. It was the signal of her surrender—a giving into what he had planned, even if she didn't know what that was.

When he broke his lip lock, her head wobbled a bit, her eyes a little drugged.

He glanced over at Carson, the one Dominant in the room he believed would understand what he needed to do. She had to recast that final piece if they were ever to find peace together. There was one thing he hadn't tried with her—and it was time.

He put a little distance between himself and Charlotte.

"Carson."

The man nodded once and stepped forward.

Chapter Seven

Charlotte shivered at the zing of leather running through belt loops. The sound always had that effect on her. Sometimes her response was fear. Sometimes anticipation. Except, when Carson removed his belt and handed it to Richard, her belly hollowed out. Nothing inside her came up.

Wayne Trembill had changed her long ago. She hadn't seen him for over two years, yet the ingrained pattern of his damage remained. First, indignation arose. Then fear. Then … emptiness. With a snap of his fingers, he could turn her into a shell.

Richard's large hand clasped over the belt in Carson's outstretched hand.

Carson didn't let go of it. One side of his mouth inched up. "This is a Forzieri. Italian leather."

"Of course it is." Richard's face remained unreadable.

Carson sliced his eyes her way. "So, make it good." He dropped his hold, stepped backward, and nodded once.

More sounds slipped through a growing haze. The scrape of a chair that Sarah brought over to her Master. With a thunk, it settled upright, and she gave Charlotte a small smile. A bit of encouragement, perhaps?

Derek dragged over two chairs, the screech of their legs on the tile echoing against the high ceilings of the chamber. Derek straddled one backward and tipped it forward, his face as serious as a funeral.

Carson took the other, swinging it so he could face her. He settled himself, adjusting his jacket, then swung his foot over a knee. Casual, like he was watching a football game.

Alexander remained standing behind them. His face was as still as ever, his eyes as blue as a glacial lake boring down on her.

Richard's hand grasped her chin and yanked her gaze to him. "So. You believe Wayne has something over me?"

What? "No. I—"

"No? One look at him, and you still believe he could harm you? Get in our way?"

Finally, something broke through the nothingness. Shame, and it spread to every corner of her body. "I …" She couldn't finish the sentence because the answer would have been "yes."

Men's shouting broke through the blood rushing in her ears. Marcos sauntered in, dragging Wayne inside by the lapels. But at least they were alone. His two goons were gone.

Wayne sported a bruised cheek, the smug look gone.

"Unhand me." Spluttering, eyes furious, face red, Wayne still felt he could do something? With those men surrounding him? Unlikely, her brain delivered. But that rising ache between her legs? Vanished.

Richard was right. Somewhere deep inside, she believed Wayne could still get to her.

Marcos pushed him forward. "Sit." He pointed at a chair. When Wayne didn't move, Marcos roughly pushed him into it. At least it was a good distance from where she and her Master stood.

"Hey. Watch yourself," Wayne growled.

She swallowed hard. This scene was surreal as if she was on the outside looking in.

Familiar faces surrounded her. Not a single person was unknown to her. How much time had passed? Did the place empty that quickly? Then again, when the Dominants in the room wanted something to happen, it did.

"Thought you were taking out the trash," Richard said calmly to Marcos.

Wayne tried to spin. "Fuck this. I'm leaving."

"I said sit your ass down." Sat him down again like he was in the naughty corner. "Wouldn't want to violate the restraining order, would you? Five hundred feet."

"There's no such—"

"There will be in about twenty more minutes."

Richard glanced over at Carson.

Carson lifted one shoulder. "Guess it pays to know an attorney."

Derek smirked. "And judges."

Restraining orders meant little to someone like Wayne.

She'd had them on him before, and they hadn't worked. What were they thinking? What was Marcos thinking? Bringing Wayne there at all?

Marcos looked straight at Richard. Something unspoken passed between the two of them.

"Make him pay," Marcos finally said.

Richard nodded once. He then settled into the chair and patted his knees.

A spanking, seriously?

"Go ahead. Roll your eyes at me," he smiled at her and held the belt up. "Only one thing can stop this, and you know it. Tell me what it is."

She tipped her chin, not understanding. *Oh.* "My safeword." Something she didn't have with Wayne.

"Very good."

Two small words that instantly filled her with warmth. She settled across his lap, her ass up in the air. Strong legs and a hard erection pressed against her stomach. Such a familiar setting, yet not. Still, as if on cue, her legs ached to spread. Despite the emptiness in her soul, one thing remained. Her mind may have emptied, but her body responded to being handled by him.

He placed his hand on her neck. His voice was even—easy. "What's your safe word, Charlotte?"

She blanked and glanced up. Caught the concentration on his face. Steffan, Laurent, and Sarah hovered nearby. Their faces, too, were unreadable.

Marcos strode over to her, knelt, and brushed the hair off her damp forehead. He shook his head slowly and tsked. "Your Master asked you a question."

A sound slap on her ass, and air flew out of her lungs. It dislodged something from her brain. "Yes. Yes, sir. Diamond."

It was a word she'd uttered only one other time. Now, it sat on the tip of her tongue, waiting in case she needed to stop the action.

"Remember it, Charlotte." A slice of panic cut through her sternum. They were words he'd uttered many times to her. Usually, they comforted. But today wasn't a typical day.

Then, the belt came down. She cried out. She hadn't expected him to start so hard.

"Count," he gritted out.

She let her head fall, her hair covering her face. "One."

Wayne's sick laughter echoed. God dammit, she shuddered in response.

"Just breathe," Marcos whispered into her hair. "Remember who you are. Where you are." He rose, and the view of his shoes disappeared. His footfalls grew distant.

Another blow to her ass, and she puffed out, "Two."

Another crack resounded through the room. And it hurt. God, it hurt. He wasn't being careful with her. He wasn't striking her in one place and moving on to the other.

"Th-three." Her nose ran, and twin tears ran down her cheeks until they hovered on her chin.

She gripped the chair leg with one hand, his strong calf with the other. Warmth from his body seeped through. She tried to tune into the heat from his thighs, anything to get away from feeling like she was back in the past. Back to when Wayne laughed at her—at her pain.

As he continued to whip her with the belt, her back

arched to get away from the fiery sting.

She wanted to surrender to Richard, give everything to him. Her Master expected nothing from her that didn't also help her.

But Wayne was there. *Watching*.

The belt came down on her, snapping like a firecracker against her flesh. She didn't know how long it went on, just chased that moment when the pain would morph into what she knew lay on the other side.

"Breathe," she said to herself. She gulped in air and let it out in a rush.

There was a moment when the sting turned. She'd first shrink from it. Then she'd grow desperate to lean into the burn. The sensation would build to a crescendo, and then, inexplicably, she'd be sliding down the other side of it, a delicious rising of pure pleasure.

God, she needed that pivotal moment. That was when she knew she was his, and he was hers. It was as if they met in the middle of a dance floor, bodies clashing together in pure ecstasy.

But it wasn't coming even as her clit began to wake up.

She couldn't forget that all those people were watching her get punished for—for what? For remembering the torture that Wayne had put her through?

No, for believing it could happen again.

But her Master wouldn't let that happen. Even if the man was sitting five hundred feet from her, and she and Richard were the only other people in the room.

She writhed a little trying to change her position and get a little friction against that growing ache between her legs.

But Richard held her firmly with one hand while the other continued to rain blows.

So much warred inside her. She was growing wet. She was scared.

A shudder ran through her, and she couldn't stay still, even with his tight grip keeping her in place.

"Who do you take this pain for?" Richard asked calmly.

"You. Master." She loved this man setting her ass on fire.

Her Master would do anything for her, and she for him. And he *was* doing something for her even though her mind couldn't have formed words for what that something was.

Her body shifted again under another blow. Her nipples, now hard peaks, rubbed against his trouser pant legs. But it wasn't enough, and she groaned in frustration. Her clit began to throb,

"One more, il mio tesoro," he whispered.

It would be the hardest. It always was. The leather came down on the tenderest part of her ass. Her legs kicked, and she bucked as the fire nearly consumed her.

She panted, her chin now wobbling. The floor under her gaze was wet with her tears.

Richard let the belt clatter to the ground. His hand left her back and fisted her hair anew. He lifted her head. "Look at them. All of them."

So many eyes on her. Assessing her.

"Do you think anything can happen to you here?"

"Plenty," she said with a tease in her voice.

His eyebrows furrowed. Okay, not what he wanted to hear. But it was true.

Alexander's blue eyes bore down on her. Carson hadn't moved an inch. But Derek leaned forward, his arms crossed across the back of the chair. His eyes glistened with something. Pride. That was what she saw.

She shifted her gaze. Sarah, Steffan, and Laurent stood as a group on the other side of the room, their faces still, though Laurent's glee couldn't be contained. And Marcos, the man who rescued her from Wayne all those years ago, stood next to the man, still guarding him.

She had so many people in her corner. Nothing horrible could happen to her there. Her brain knew that.

But she couldn't stop her inner vigilance with Wayne in the room. His shoulders were hunched from defeat, yet the same judge-y disgust colored his face.

Richard slapped her flesh, and she cried out as flames seemed to lick at her skin. He slid a finger down her ass crack to her folds. "So much pain. Yet ..." His finger swirled in all the wet. Of course, her body would respond to his handling that way. "Who is this for?"

Wayne chuffed, and Derek's chair slammed to the ground. His eyes never left Charlotte, though.

Wayne shifted uncomfortably, perhaps waiting to be jumped. So strange. That was how she'd always felt. She'd walk by him on the couch, never knowing if she'd be yanked to the ground, told to crawl up between his knees. Make him come.

She'd once held a plate of nachos as the men watched a game. They'd tripped her, so she ended up over their laps, the cheese and chips going everywhere. They'd held her there for long minutes, all their hands on her, tickling her, trying to strip her …

But it was all a game to them, wasn't it? To humiliate her?

"You. Only you," she whispered. The words felt hollow even though they were true.

He thrust his finger in and out of her pussy. She was so damp; the sounds of her arousal filled the room. "All this for me."

He moved to her ass and thrust that thick digit, wet with her juice, inside her. "And this?"

She gasped. He was never that harsh, usually warming her up slowly. But his hard erection pressed against her belly, his grip on her ribs tight and controlled, told her his patience was thinning.

"You," she barely whispered.

"Who do you come for?" Richard growled, his pelvis arching slightly up at her. His desire was evident. He wanted her, too.

"You. Always, my Master."

There wasn't much Charlotte was certain of in life, but his desire for her was one of them. Yet he'd hold himself back for hours if needed.

His finger moved in and out. He then began to really torture her.

For more long minutes, he brought her to the edge again and again with his hands. He'd pinch the welts on her ass, then move his fingers in and out of her pussy, her ass. Going back and forth until she was nothing but raw need and electricity and didn't care who was in the room.

He brought her to the state he wanted: needing to be

fucked—hard.

"P-please," she begged.

"Don't you dare hold back." His thumb pressed against her clit as his middle finger curled inside her.

She let go, shuddering on his lap, nearly falling off if it wasn't for his strong grip around her torso. Her hands wrapped around one chair leg and one of his legs as she rode her release.

He let her come?

Wayne's sick laugh ruined it. "All these guys next?"

Her gaze shot up, panic setting in.

Marcos, standing nearby, clocked Wayne on the side of his head. Wayne yelped and folded over his legs, spluttering and swearing.

Marcos dipped one chin toward Richard. "You get next time."

Richard cupped her chin and lifted her gaze. "Look at him. Really look."

Under hooded, tired eyes, the man who'd ruined her stared at her. His snarl, teeth stained with blood, almost didn't look real. He was like a cartoon character.

She waited for the shudder, the warning that the fear was still there, mocking her from the inside. It didn't come. Maybe because she'd just come, her insides still fluttering a bit?

Perhaps it was because she was splayed across the lap of her master, safe.

Or perhaps it was because not a single person looked at Wayne. All eyes were trained on her. They didn't care about him. At that moment, the full weight of her control, her agency, clicked into place. Those men—and women— were there for her. *Richard* was there for her.

She glanced back at Wayne, and the only word she could think of shot into her consciousness.

"Broken," she whispered. He was so broken.

She twisted to peer up at Richard, her Master, her love, and he let her.

His lips twitched in a hidden smile. But then he turned serious. He ran his hands over her ass slowly, reigniting the burn. God, she loved him. If she could crawl into his chest and stay there forever, she would.

"Master?" she whispered. "Will you …"

"Yes, tesoro."

She hadn't even told him what she wanted—to be claimed once more. Right then. Oh, she'd been collared, played with, *served* in only the way she needed, which was to serve him. But not in front of the only person on the planet who'd tried to interrupt that full commitment. It was time for Wayne's hold on her to end.

Richard grasped her around the waist and yanked her up. He dragged the chair so the back faced the crowd. He spun her so she faced it—and all the people gathered around.

So many people in the room, all dead opposite of Wayne's crowd. Carson, Derek, Marcos, Steffan, Sarah, Laurent, and Alexander all watched her as if they hadn't a care in the world, as if they didn't have any other place to be.

Only Laurent looked a little undone. He licked his lips, his hands twitching by his side as if he wished to join in.

Where were the other women?

Sarah was there, her face as placid as ever. But London, Samantha, and Isabella, all mated to the other men, were not. Why did she know an army of guards likely had them sequestered some other place?

Because that was what those men—and Sarah—did. At the first sign of danger, they protected.

"Wayne Trembill," Richard called. "You don't get to watch me fuck her. Because that's what I want. And I always get what I want where Charlotte is concerned."

Marcos leaned down and yanked Wayne up to stand before spinning the chair, so Wayne sat facing away from everyone, forced to stare at a wall. "Listen and learn," Marcos said to him.

Amazingly, Wayne let it happen. Perhaps he knew he was outnumbered. The only way out was to fight, and there was no chance of winning.

His suit coat bunched around his waist, the back of his greasy head a few hundred feet away. She almost giggled at the sight. He really did look like he faced the naughty corner. Like a toddler who needed to learn a lesson. It was … sad.

Richard pinched the bruised skin on her ass, and she yelped. "Grab the chair seat and spread those legs."

The rasp in his voice had grown, likely from playing with her and yet having to hold his own pleasure back. There was a line, however, that once crossed meant he could ravage her on the Capitol Steps in front of the Capitol police without a care.

She leaned over, her hand curling around the wooden back, and widened her stance.

He brought his lips close to her ear. "And right now, my little girl, you're going to give it all to me. Let him hear you. Tell him how much you belong to me."

Something shifted in her as if the building blocks of who she thought she was had rearranged somehow.

She didn't settle on that thought long as a finger pressed into her ass. Oh, my God. Is that what he meant? They'd not done much anal play before—and never with witnesses.

His hand were still wet from her coming all over him, but Jesus … The stretch was just that side of pain.

The zing of a zipper being lowered was next. "Will you let me here, *tesoro*? Let me do anything to you?" He curled his finger inside her ever so slightly.

She could utter her safe word, but did she want to?

With her Master, she always had choices. She stared at the back of Wayne's head. That man thought he could take anything from her. But Richard didn't have to take. She gave him whatever he desired. That was the life she wanted—where she got to choose.

But this …

She peered under her arm and caught one of his thick brows arching above his beautiful dark eye. She could stop it. But then they'd be back to square one, wouldn't they?

"I will not ask twice."

She blinked at him. "Anything. Always." Then she faced the chair back and widened her legs a bit more, though that made her ass tighten around his intruding finger. She clenched a little around it.

Richard murmured, amused. "Careful, there. You want me going slow." Still, he inserted a second finger, and she gasped. "I don't suppose ..."

Sarah strode forward, instantly enveloping Charlotte in her scent, an expensive French perfume. "Of course, Master R."

The click of a bottle top opening. Lube. Of course, their community was prepared for anything at any time.

Cool gel touched her backside. Richard's eager, slick fingers returned to massaging her tight hole.

He slipped in two, then three fingers, pressing and probing until she whimpered.

His whole body moved closer, the head of his cock nudging at her opening. He was going to be too big. Her knuckles whitened from their clutch on the chair seat. "I love you, Charlotte." He pressed inside, and she clenched hard. "Now, breathe me in. Take me in."

He gripped her hips and pressed forward, breaching the tight muscle. She muffled a scream and tried to still her legs, but they danced against the burn.

"Christ, so good," he hissed, his shirt tails brushing against her bare ass.

He pulled back a little and then pressed in again. His fingers dug into her harder and tried to hold her still. But she couldn't. It hurt so much.

She kept her eyes on the floor, mentally tracing the patterns on the tile. Breathe, she had to remember to breathe. He started slow, long strokes as his hands ran up and down her spine like he was petting a horse he was riding. Using her.

His touch was always possessive, loving even when inflicting pain.

The message was clear. She belonged to him, and he'd use her, love her, play with her any way he liked. He wouldn't let anyone or anything touch her—even the man with his back to her. Now, she *knew* it.

She wouldn't want anything else ever again. She'd let the burn take her over. Burn her to ashes as he used her.

He hissed behind her, then gave her ass a hard spank. "Fuck, you're beautiful. You should see your ass spread wide to take me." She was just so full.

He pulled out and then went back in again. That time, her body seemed to get it. It still hurt but not as much. She felt his hair, his root, his entire possession at that moment, and a trickle of juice ran down her inner thigh.

The man raised so many things in her, time and time again. Taboo. Forbidden. Filthy. All words that danced in her mind at what they were doing. God, she wanted it. With her Master, she wanted everything.

Her forearms fell to the seat of the chair, and she began to push back to greet his thrusts. Her breath was now freely blowing out of her lungs in puffs. She arched her back more and lifted her chin high. She'd grown half mad with lust, half unbalanced with discomfort.

Her Master bent down, nipping at her shoulder. "That's a good girl. Love what I'm doing to you."

He didn't have to direct her around that. She did, even though she might be split in two, her hips bruised with fingerprints from his tight grip.

He picked up the pace until he was truly fucking her. His balls slapped against her ass, and her clit throbbed anew.

The pleasure-pain combination blanked her mind.

Memories, feelings … all got lost in the maelstrom. Only one thing, like a mantra, kept beating inside her: *His. His. His.*

Her legs trembled. She was going to fall, pitch over the chair. But the drumbeat grew louder and louder until she was chanting aloud. "His. His."

A slap on her ass had her yelp. It jostled his cock inside her, a knife of pain arrowing through her center. "Whose?" He thrust hard until she had to catch herself before her head slammed into the chair.

"Yours. Only yours," she called out. To prove it, she clenched inside, sucking on his cock a little with her internal muscles. She didn't know where she got the strength. Her legs shook with fatigue.

"Everything inside you is mine," he hissed, and then he let go. His cock jerked inside her, filling her with his release.

It was such a powerful thing to have a man become undone for a few seconds. And at that moment, as if he had passed on a message, she got it. He'd built her strength with every test, with every experience. Every time she gave up her control, her power to her Master, it grew inside her. To give him more, she had to *be* more.

Her past would never leave her, but it could no longer touch her the same way. Because she wasn't the same person anymore. The lost little girl was Richard's Submissive, lover, friend, and soon … wife.

Richard eased out and lifted her to standing. She nearly crumbled into his chest. He held her there as she caught her breath. Sweat had seeped through his shirt, and his belly was tight from exertion.

He pulled her face back, one hand pushing hair roughly off her cheeks. "Who do you take pain for?" His voice was nothing more than a rasp.

"You. Only you."

And, if he'd let her—and Charlotte already knew her Master *wouldn't* let her—she'd take out the trash herself.

Chapter Eight

Four months later

The wedding cake hit her tongue, and she nearly orgasmed on the spot. Chocolate base with a raspberry filling and a chocolate, cinnamon-infused ganache topping sprinkled with nuts? Nothing tasted better—except perhaps for the man standing before her.

Her blue silk dress, the very one she'd modeled months ago on her independence day, as she'd dubbed it, rustled as she stepped back to gaze into his eyes. She licked her bottom lip to entice Richard as much as to lick off the last bit of chocolate.

He winked. "My little vixen."

"And beautiful in that dress." Laurent chuckled and sidled up to them. "I wonder who designed it? It looks as if it were made for you." He kissed her on the cheek.

"Congratulations, you two."

Champagne glasses clinked in the background, and light chatter mixed in with the beautiful cello and violin music from the quartet in the corner of the Accendos Library. It was the perfect place for their wedding reception, with all their friends gathered around. Alexander, Rebecca, Laurent, Sarah, Steffan, Marcos and Isabella, Carson and London, Jonathan and Christiana, Derek and Samantha with their two adorable children—all dressed in beautiful brocades and silks and tuxedos, all there for them. Smiling. Happy.

Laurent nodded once at Richard. "Everything's ready for you."

"Ready?" she asked.

Richard took her plate and set it down by the half-demolished cake. "Time for a wedding present."

"Being your wife is enough. Now, I have all the titles," she teased. Submissive, owned, collared, and now, legally bound as man and wife.

He grasped her hand anyway and pulled her away from the cake table, leading her up the circular staircase to the balcony—one of Alexander's favorite spots to watch the usual playtime below. Today it was empty. She'd rarely been up there, which is why when Richard cracked open a long bookcase to reveal it was a door, she stopped short.

"A secret room?" she gasped.

"The Master's private library."

She peeked inside. "I never knew."

"Most don't."

Two antique leather club chairs sat before a fireplace, lit with a dozen ivory pillar candles giving off a soft glow. Floor-to-ceiling bookshelves holding leather-bound volumes lined the walls, and a small writing desk stood in the corner.

The door clicked shut behind her. Richard spun her into his arms, the fabric of her dress rustling against his trouser legs. "Mmm, you smell so good," he murmured into her hair. "Happy?"

"Beyond." Words hadn't yet been invented for the joy that danced inside her.

After the fashion show, she'd felt soft, peaceful, wanting nothing more than to nestle into Richard's arms and be quiet. Needing to just be near him. Not talk. Not do anything. And that was what they'd done. Slowly, she resumed her life. Working with Isabella on Garden Grace projects, making dinners for Richard. But it felt new. *She* was new.

She still had the odd nightmare leading up to their wedding, but her heartbeat barely registered the nightly intrusions. She'd simply bury her face in Richard's neck, feel his arms band her to him, still asleep but always reaching for her. The images would fade to smoke, and bit by bit, as the days passed, she hardly thought of what her life was like before him.

Now, fluttery anticipation had grown in her belly. There was so much more to feel, think, and do. She'd broken through a gate she hadn't realized had her hemmed in all that time.

She inhaled his scent mixing with the dusty smell of old books and leather. "So good," she murmured.

He pulled back, his dark eyes clear and bright. "About that present."

He settled her into a chair.

After shrugging off his jacket, he got on bended knee—a position she rarely saw him in. Not even when he proposed. Rather, he stood before her, towering over her as he asked the question.

He held out his arm. "Unbutton my cuff."

Oh, perhaps they were starting their honeymoon early. She was ready, a twinge going off between her legs. The small buttons gave way without a fight, revealing the dark hair that dusted his skin. The twinge? It rose to a burn. No aphrodisiac could have a greater effect than merely touching Richard's strong forearms.

His gaze never left her face. "Roll it up."

He turned his bare arm over, and she sucked in a quick breath. A brand new tattoo, a Phoenix, a little red and raw, stared up at her. Her name was etched underneath in a beautiful script.

"It's you," he said. "You've burned and risen every time, mi tesoro. And I love you for it. Now, I carry with me your courage."

She traced the tiny wings of the bird. Tiny, inked feathers graced two large wings that appeared in mid-flight. Its large eyes stared right at her. "She's beautiful."

"Like you."

She raised her lashes and drank in his beautiful eyes. "Uncanny."

His brows pinched together in question. She also had a surprise. But how could she tell him what she'd done? First, she hadn't talked to him about it before going ahead. That would have ruined the surprise. She only hoped he'd be pleased.

Her breath quickened. "I have something for you, too."

She'd wanted to reveal it to him when they reached their honeymoon destination—two weeks on Makepeace Island in Australia. They were to leave immediately after the reception. She'd prayed she could keep it secret until then. But now was better.

She sucked in a long breath and stood. "Please forgive me that I didn't get permission first."

"You can stand." He chuckled and righted himself.

"No, I mean …" She tried to turn around, but her dress got caught on the chair and his legs. She ended up pitching into the chair. "Ooof." Clumsy much?

His arm banded around the waist and righted her. "Trying to run away?" His deep growl flashed an image of the big bad wolf in her mind. She wouldn't mind being chased by him.

"Can you help me with my dress?"

"Charlotte." His tone was both warning and questioning. He swiped his finger along the back of her neck, sending a shudder down her spine. "Attempting to seduce me?"

"No. I mean, yes, always, but … please?" She had to look over her shoulder to catch his face. He had her pressed to his chest. She grabbed fistfuls of her dress and tried to yank the hemline up.

He let go of her and stepped backward. "Eager. Need help?" Once more, his laughter reached her ears. He wasn't mad, rather amused.

"Please. I have something to show you—"

"On your ass?"

A giggle erupted from her own throat. "Yes, actually."

The energy in the room dropped. Though teasing, he'd guessed the truth. She'd surprised him, all right. *Move quickly.* Her dress would be wrinkled beyond belief, and everyone downstairs would think they were up here having sex, but really, who cared?

Now, with her arms full of fabric, her legs were free to move her around. She pushed her butt out.

"No panties. Had I known, I might have had us up here earlier," his deep voice said. "And had I known about this ..." His fingertip traced the crescent moon tattoo on her cheek. She couldn't see it now, but that morning in the mirror, it also had looked a little red and raw, given it was only a week old.

"It's a sign of rebirth," she said quickly. "So, when you ..."

"Spank you, fuck you, I'll see it." His voice matched his raw words.

"And know you're always bringing me back," she added quickly. *What* to get inked into her skin took long thought. Whenever she thought of Richard, however, that image kept coming back to mind. Like a moon lighting a traveler's path, Richard always showed her the way, and she'd always found herself someplace better.

He drew the fabric fall back down to cover her. *Oh, no.* He didn't like it.

He moved her to face him. That time, his eyes were different—misted and wet, and his lids slightly hooded.

"Surprised?" she asked softly.

He nodded once.

"Happy?"

"Beyond," he whispered.

She grabbed both his hands and brought them up to her lips. "These hands can do anything to me. Not because you have the ability, but because I trust them. I trust every part of you." But it was more than that, wasn't it? He was deserving—and she was, as well. "Any man can stand between the dark and me. But you loved *my* darkness."

"I have—and always will—love every part of you." Rough edges tinged his voice.

She dripped her chin and closed her eyes. "I am here for you. Always."

"Mio tesoro." His lips found hers, and she lost herself in his kiss. Warm light filled her body. So, that was what peace felt like.

He'd often called her *my treasure*. But for the first time, she felt like one bone deep. Not just because he loved her. Because she'd finally let herself accept it—fully.

Thank you for reading **Finally, His**, *an Elite Doms of Washington* novelette collection!

The Elite Doms of Washington series contains six full-length books and two novellas. You'll find the reading order on the next page or visit ElizabethSaFleur.com here.

You can also join her email newsletter on her site, ensuring you'll never miss a new release

ABOUT THE AUTHOR

Elizabeth SaFleur writes award-winning, luscious romance from 28 wildlife-filled acres, hikes in her spare time and is a certifiable tea snob. Find out more about Elizabeth on her web site at www.ElizabethSaFleur or join her private Facebook group, Elizabeth's Playroom. Follow her on TikTok (@ElizabethSaFleurAuthor) and Instagram (@ElizabethLoveStory), too.

ALSO BY ELIZABETH SAFLEUR

Erotic romance with BDSM:
Elite
Holiday Ties
Untouchable
Perfect
Riptide
Lucky
Fearless
Invincible

Femme Domme:
The White House Gets A Spanking
Spanking the Senator

Steamy Contemporary romance:
Tough Road
Tough Luck
Tough Break
Tough Love

Sexy rom-coms:
The Sassy Nanny Dilemma
It Was All The Pie's Fault
It Was All the Cat's Fault
It Was All the Daisy's Fault

Short story collections:
Finally, Yours
Finally, His
Finally, Mine

Made in the USA
Middletown, DE
16 October 2023

40881539R00142